Martha's home

Ida Kate's home

Big Creek

Kansas & Union Pacific Railroad

Schoolhouse

IDA KATE'S WORLD
Kansas in 1878

Hays City

RIDDLE OF THE PRAIRIE BRIDE

᠗

by

Kathryn Reiss

AmericanGirl™

SCHOLASTIC INC.

New York Toronto London Auckland Sydney
Mexico City New Delhi Hong Kong Buenos Aires

PERMISSIONS & PICTURE CREDITS
The following individuals and organizations have generously given permission to reprint
illustrations contained in "A Peek into the Past": p. 155—Denver Public Library, Western History
Collection; pp. 156-157—poster, Library of Congress, Rare Books Division; railway station,
CORBIS/Alexander Alland, Sr.; catalog cover and photo of woman, from the Thomas Parks
Collection #4464, Southern Historical Collection, Wilson Library, The University of North
Carolina at Chapel Hill; farmer, Kansas State Historical Society; pp. 158-159—sod house, Nebraska
State Historical Society, Solomon D. Butcher Collection; grasshopper, photo by Mike Buesing;
Hays City street, Kansas State Historical Society; pp. 160-161—sewing circle, Kansas State
Historical Society; factory, CORBIS; *The Prairie Is My Garden* by Harvey Dunn, South Dakota
Art Museum Collection. Photo of author on p. 163 by Tom Strychacz.

ISBN 0-439-39874-6

12 11 10 9 8 7 6 5 4 3 2 1   2 3 4 5 6 7/0

Printed in the U.S.A.   23
First Scholastic printing, April 2002

Cover and Map Illustrations: Paul Bachem
Line Art: Laszlo Kubinyi

For Maria and Geoffrey,
and especially India Reiss,
great-great-granddaughter of a real *Ida Kate*

And special thanks to
Lynn and Frank Deming,
who shared family stories of Kansas

TABLE OF CONTENTS

CHAPTER I

HERE COMES THE BRIDE

Twelve-year-old Ida Kate Deming squinted down the tracks as far as she could see, but there was no train coming. The April afternoon was warm and it was heaven to be outdoors without her shawl, though Papa predicted the fine weather wouldn't hold. A "false spring," he called it. Still, it felt wonderful, and seemed a good omen. She hopped one foot to the next, then made herself stop and stand ladylike; it wouldn't do to spoil a good first impression by acting like a baby with a grasshopper down its back. But she was so excited—and she and Papa had been waiting so long!

People all around them were peering down the tracks. The arrival of the train was always a thrilling event in Hays City. Their little Kansas town, once just an outpost near Fort Hays along Big Creek, was now a bustling place. Settlers had been coming for more than a decade—first to

the fort, which had been established back in 1867 to protect railway builders from Indian attacks, and then to the
growing town nearby. The railway tracks now stretched
all the way to California! The train brought goods and
supplies to Hays City, as well as plenty of businessmen,
farmers, and families from the eastern states. Some immigrants came from as far away as Europe. They stopped in
Hays City, Kansas—and stayed.

And soon—so soon!—there would be a new settler.
Ida Kate, still looking anxiously down the empty tracks,
reached out one arm and linked it through Papa's. "Papa?
Could it be that the train has derailed somewhere along
the line—?"

"Nonsense, Ida Kate. We've been waiting only twenty
minutes." Papa's voice was calm, as it almost always was,
but Ida Kate noticed how he kept stroking his dark
beard—a sure sign he was agitated. It seemed they had
been waiting for *hours* already, though when Papa reached
into his vest, his pocket watch confirmed it had been
only twenty minutes.

*Twenty minutes, and three days, and six months, and two
years,* thought Ida Kate, shoving her fists down deep
into the pockets of her best dress. Twenty minutes since
they'd been waiting here at the train depot. Three days
since they'd received the telegram and gone into a whirlwind of preparations to get the house all ready. Six
months since Papa first started looking for a new bride.

And two years since the death of Ida Kate's adored mother and Papa's beloved wife—a tragic loss that had thrown their little family into a well of grief that neither father nor daughter thought they'd ever climb out of again.

Ida Kate's mother, Eleanor Deming, always frail, had died after a long winter of illness. She'd grown thin and couldn't eat, and she slept all the time. Then, during a terrible blizzard, she developed a raging fever that left her delirious, but it had been impossible to fetch the doctor from Hays City. A ride that took less than an hour over the prairie in fine weather could take a full day— or longer—when swirling snow turned the path invisible. And so Mama had died with her husband and daughter by her side. They buried her later in the graveyard on the prairie where small headstones already marked the final resting places of the two babies, born after Ida Kate, who had not lived more than a few days. *Adored Mother, Beloved Wife* read the gravestone. Gone from their lives but not forgotten, Mama was now an angel watching over her—Ida Kate was sure of it. She often talked to Mama. She felt certain Mama could hear her.

Ida Kate had learned—she'd *had* to learn—to do all the housekeeping herself. Papa's long hours of work in the fields and barn left him no time to run the home. Ida Kate's days, which had been so happily spent at the new one-room schoolhouse four miles from their farm, now were spent on chores: milking cows, churning butter, tending the garden, sewing clothing for herself and Papa from the fabric they bought at the general store, and doing laundry—now *that* was the job Ida Kate hated most of all. Even when Mama was alive, Ida Kate had hated it—boiling the endless vats of water and spending the day outdoors washing the clothes with homemade soap, wringing them out, stretching them across the line to dry, then spending the following day heating and reheating heavy irons to press out the wrinkles . . . *Ugh*. It was thankless and never-ending work because the clothes just got soiled again.

All the housework meant that Ida Kate had to miss more and more school. Sometimes Martha Ruppenthal, Ida Kate's friend who lived on the property adjoining the Demings', would walk over to visit Ida Kate and keep her updated on what was happening at school. And for a while after Mama died, Miss Artemia Butler, the schoolteacher, rode over to Ida Kate's house nearly every week, ostensibly to tutor Ida Kate in arithmetic or geography. She always brought gifts of jam or crocks of butter, and once even a length of calico cloth from the general store, which her father owned. But when it became clear that Miss Butler was more interested in winning Papa's affection than in tutoring Ida Kate, Papa managed to be out in the fields whenever Miss Butler came to call, and soon the visits stopped.

Ida Kate and her father had learned to muddle along without Mama, but life just wasn't the same. They both missed Mama's quiet presence, her stories in the evening around the fire, her cheerful touches of flowers in jugs to brighten the dark interior of the sod house.

Yes, there were plenty of sad times on the prairie, but there had been good times, too. And now there would be many more good times, Ida Kate felt sure—not to mention the chance to go back to school!—once her father's new bride, a widowed lady from Massachusetts, finally arrived.

She's coming, Mama! Today—on the train, IF it ever gets here!

Ida Kate pulled the telegram out of her dress pocket and read the message over once more:

REGRET LONG DELAY STOP WILL LEAVE FOR KANSAS TOMORROW STOP ARRIV- ING HAYS CITY APRIL 12 STOP EAGER TO MEET YOU AT LAST STOP BEST REGARDS CAROLINE FAIRCHILD

"It's so *short,* Papa," Ida Kate had complained three days ago after the delivery rider galloped off and she and her father read the message. Papa had sent the train ticket a full two months earlier, but there had been no word from Mrs. Fairchild. "It doesn't say anything at all about why she hasn't written for so long."

"There could be many reasons," her father had replied. "Maybe the baby took sick. Maybe she had second thoughts about journeying west to marry a man she doesn't even know!" He shook his head. "I wouldn't blame her if she did have reservations. It's a very big step to take. I think she must be a brave woman."

"We're going to like her, Papa, I just know it. Her letters sound so friendly and kind," Ida Kate had said, and a thrill of excitement jumped in her belly now as she saw the first puff of smoke far down the tracks.

"She's coming! Papa!"

Papa cleared his throat as if he were practicing to make a speech. "Ahem, ahem, ahem . . ." He stroked his black beard into place.

Watching him, Ida Kate had to smile. He was more nervous even than she! But, of course, Mrs. Fairchild was coming to be his *bride,* not his stepmother. Ida Kate reached up to straighten his collar. "Now you look the perfect gentleman, Papa," she told him. "Do stop worrying!"

"Who's worrying?" he asked, peering down the tracks, his dark eyes anxious.

Of course he was anxious. Ida Kate suspected that Mrs. Fairchild was feeling anxious herself. After all, Papa and Mrs. Fairchild, who had never met, planned to marry within weeks if all went well. Yet why shouldn't it go well? Martha Ruppenthal's father had also sent east for a "mail-order bride" and was very happy with Martha's stepmother, a friendly German woman named Margaretha. And now Martha and the nine-year-old twins, Jimmy and Johnny, had two new little brothers and a baby sister.

Now I'll have a brother, too, Ida Kate thought as she watched the black speck in the distance turn into a real train, eating the miles across the prairie just as it had been chugging along for days and days now, all the way from Massachusetts. For Caroline Fairchild, a widow whose husband had been wounded in the War Between the States and never fully recovered, had a son. The baby boy was just a year old, she'd written. Ida Kate was eager to be a big sister. To have a mother in the house. To be a *family* again.

Ida Kate was wearing her best going-to-church dress. She had washed her long brown hair and braided it as neatly as possible, frowning into the small spotty mirror over her bureau as she tied the ribbons into bows. Next year, Papa said, she would be old enough to put her hair up. But today she looked just as she always did—thin, freckled face, big gray eyes like Mama's—only just a bit neater than usual. She wanted to look presentable for Caroline Fairchild. She wanted to look pretty.

Ida Kate felt sure that her father's new bride would be pretty, although Caroline Fairchild had described herself modestly as *tall and thin, with auburn hair and greenish eyes* in one of her letters. *I have been told I have the look of a cat,* she'd written, *although I cannot be around cats without sneezing!*

That was the only bad thing about this new bride, Ida Kate reflected. Papa said all the cats would have to live in the barn once Mrs. Fairchild arrived—even Ida Kate's favorite kitten, Millie. But Ida Kate told herself Millie wouldn't mind *too* much. The barn was warm.

The roaring train was now a presence no one could ignore. From that tiny black speck in the distance, the train had become a huge, looming monster. Roaring up the tracks, it chugged and puffed, clattering along the rails and sending up clouds of black smoke from its smokestack. The iron wheels screeched as the brakeman applied the brakes. People moved back on the platform. Other people came running out of shops and boardinghouses to meet the train. Hays City's main street was only about a block long, with the train tracks right down the center. The Kansas and Union Pacific Railroad Station, just a little red station house with a long platform, was the town's favorite meeting place when a train pulled in.

The train shuddered to a stop, the smoke cleared, and Ida Kate found she was holding her breath as the passengers started pushing through the doors. Would she and Papa recognize Mrs. Fairchild from her description? What would she be wearing? They hadn't thought to ask. *Before the War, when I lived with my family in North Carolina,* Mrs. Fairchild had written in one of her letters, *I had an eye for fashion and style as much as any young girl. But in this decade since the War, times have been very hard indeed. I've had no money and little inclination to indulge in fripperies. I am afraid you will find me very plain. . . .*

Ida Kate didn't care how plain Mrs. Fairchild's dress was, so long as she had a smile on her face and a kind heart beating in her breast. Ida Kate scanned the passengers crowding off the train. Most were men. Some were soldiers. Some were cowboys. Some were farmers who meant to stake their claim to the hundred and sixty acres of prairie land granted by the government—just as Papa had done when he first came to Kansas. Their families would follow later.

Some of the passengers were rough looking, rumpled and unshaven. They would find a place to stay, Ida Kate supposed, at one of the many boardinghouses in town. Other passengers looked as if they had places to go and people to meet immediately. Their eyes scanned the crowd even as the eyes of the crowd scanned them. And then there was a woman—a lady with a baby!

"Is that Mrs. Fairchild?" asked Ida Kate, gripping Papa's arm hard.

"I don't know," Papa answered uncertainly. "She wrote she was tall—"

"But there's no other lady with a baby . . ."

The woman wasn't much taller than Ida Kate herself. Most of her hair was hidden by a stylish hat. With one arm she balanced the squirming baby on her hip, and with the other arm she struggled to carry a heavy reticule. The canvas bag bumped against her side with each step as she headed right toward Ida Kate and Papa.

"Mr. Deming?" she asked softly, stopping directly in front of them. Her voice had the lilt of a southern accent only natural in a lady born and bred in North Carolina. "Mr. Henry Deming?" The squirmy baby in her arms laughed and held out his arms.

"Indeed I am," said Papa, stepping forward. "At your service." He bowed, then reached out his hand to take the heavy bag she was carrying.

"And this lovely girl must be Ida Kate?"

"Yes," Ida Kate said, and curtsied. "Yes, ma'am, Mrs. Fairchild."

The lady smiled. "As I am sure we will become fast friends," she said, "I do hope you will call me Caroline." She shifted the baby in her arms. "And this fine fellow is Hanky. Officially Henry, but always Hanky to his nearest and dearest." The baby chortled. She brushed back a tendril of his reddish hair. Her eyes sparkled at Ida Kate and Papa. "I do declare," she said, her eyes widening as she looked past them at the bustling station and the vast prairie stretching beyond to the horizon. "Hanky, my darlin' boy, are we really here at last? I can scarcely believe this isn't a dream."

Papa threw his head back and laughed. "Well, if it is, don't wake me."

"Don't wake me, either," said Ida Kate.

CHAPTER 2

HOMECOMING

"S o this little fellow is another Henry," Papa said as they walked out of the station, followed by a porter wheeling Caroline's big wooden trunk on a handcart. "In your letters you always called him 'Hanky,' and I'd just assumed that was his given name—perhaps a family name . . ."

"No, it's really Henry," Caroline said. "But that sounds too grown up for such a tiny peanut. Of course, with some good prairie air in his lungs and some fresh farm food in his belly, he may well grow into his name."

"Papa's name is Henry Clay," Ida Kate piped up. She was walking along between Caroline and her father. "He's Henry Clay Deming the Second, and my grandfather back in Philadelphia wanted me to be a boy so that I could be Henry Clay Deming the Third. Henry Clay was a great abolitionist, you know, and fought against slavery—"

Ooops! Ida Kate broke off and pressed her lips together.

Papa shot her a frown. She'd forgotten what they'd both agreed on: no talking about the evils of slavery or the War Between the States until they got to know Mrs. Fairchild better. She had grown up as the daughter of a wealthy southern planter, and no doubt her family had owned slaves. The Demings of Philadelphia, on the other hand, had been ardent abolitionists, fighting *against* slavery. Papa himself had fought against the South and had been injured in battle at Gettysburg.

Papa was laughing now, trying to cover up Ida Kate's tactless slip. "If my father knew I was about to add another Henry to the family, I might rise up in his estimation."

When Caroline looked puzzled, Papa added, "You remember I wrote to you about the trouble with my family back in Philadelphia?"

"Oh, yes—yes of course," said Caroline.

"My grandfather wanted Papa to join the Deming law firm," Ida Kate explained, because it looked as if Caroline had forgotten. "But he and Mama wanted to come to Kansas to stake their claim. And you did, didn't you, Papa?" She grinned up at her father as they reached the horses and wagon outside the station. Papa grinned back.

Papa had left Mama and Ida Kate—only two years old at the time—living back in Philadelphia with his stern parents while he traveled to Kansas to claim his one hundred and sixty acres of land. All people who wanted to be homesteaders received land, provided they would stay for at least five years to work it. Soon Papa sent for Mama and Ida Kate. They were happy to be homesteaders, living in the house Papa built out of sod bricks, farming the land and raising cattle—making a life for themselves far away from the stifling (Papa said) society back in Philadelphia.

Now Papa helped the porter hoist the heavy trunk into the back of the wagon. Then he assisted Caroline up onto the high buckboard seat and settled baby Hanky in her lap. Ida Kate clambered into the back and made herself comfortable on top of Caroline's trunk. Papa paid the porter, tossed a coin to the boy who had held the horses while they waited at the depot, and then they were off.

Caroline Fairchild stared around her as the wagon jounced down the rutted main street of Hays City. Ida Kate tried to imagine that she, too, was seeing everything for the first time. There were cottonwood and willow trees growing along Big Creek, but hardly any grew along the hard-packed street, which was lined with a board-walk to keep people out of the dirt and mud. The north side of the street was a huddle of boardinghouses, stores, saloons, and dance halls. There was the pharmacy where Papa bought medicines for the animals and for himself and Ida Kate—throat salve, ointment for burns, castor oil.

There was the barbershop and the fancy York House Hotel. There was Sol Cohen's clothing store and Butler's General Merchandise. The south side of the street had even more saloons. You would never run out of spirits to drink in Hays City, that was for sure. Ida Kate pointed out the post office, the newspaper office, and the Leavenworth Restaurant, her voice giddy with excitement. She so hoped that Caroline Fairchild would like Hays City, that she would like the farm, and most of all that she would like the Demings. To Ida Kate, Hays City was an exciting place, and their house a cozy home—but she worried both might seem dumpy and rough to someone used to grand cities.

The road out of Hays abruptly became prairie. Caroline gasped at the expanse of open grassland. "It's so—so huge," she said. "It looks even bigger out here in the open than it did from the train. A true marvel!"

Although to Ida Kate the prairie was as familiar as the sky above, she looked out at the vista now with fresh appreciation. New green grass rippled in the wind like waves in every direction—all the way to the horizon, where the line of green met the sky. There was almost nothing to see but the rise and swell of land and grass, and then more grass. Only occasionally a little stand of bent trees, or a squat sod house and barn, or the rise of a low hill interrupted the otherwise unbroken view of the endless prairie.

"Yes, it is a marvel," agreed Papa. "Grass, grass—as far as the eye can see."

"Why, it's like an ocean!" exclaimed Caroline, and Papa chuckled. It was a good sign that Caroline could make Papa laugh, Ida Kate reflected. He hadn't laughed much since Mama died.

It was strange seeing a woman up on the seat next to Papa again. Caroline took off her traveling hat when the wind threatened to blow it away. "I'll have to get a bonnet like yours, Ida Kate," she said. "I can see now that this little hat is too impractical for the prairie." Her hair, really more of a light brown than the auburn she'd mentioned in her letter, was pulled back into a neat bun. She wore a blue serge traveling dress and neat black boots—somehow managing to look elegant even though the dress was creased and rumpled from days of travel and there was a stain on one shoulder where the baby must have drooled on her. Her eyes were wide and bright, looking more blue than green, perhaps reflecting the blue of the serge traveling suit. A faint flowery scent enveloped her.

"It's such a lovely day," Caroline said brightly to Papa, and Ida Kate leaned forward to hear. "I'd thought it would be colder here on the prairie so early in spring. But this is perfect weather!"

"Don't be fooled," Papa replied. "Kansas weather is fickle. We're bound to have more snow before the real spring is here."

"Oh, dear," said Caroline. "But I suppose life must hold its hardships . . ."

"There are plenty of hardships in Kansas," boasted Ida Kate. "Why, last year there was a tornado that came out of nowhere in the spring, and it tore down part of the Ruppenthals' fence! And a few years before that," she continued eagerly, "there was a plague of grasshoppers, wasn't there, Papa? They blew in like black clouds on the winds and landed everywhere—oh, and they were hungry! They completely ruined everybody's crops and frightened the cattle into stampeding—"

"Whoa, girl, whoa!" cried Papa, and he wasn't talking to either of the horses. "Ida Kate, my girl, you'll be terrifying our special guest before she's even set foot on our property. Let's tell Caroline the good parts of life on the prairie before we scare her away!"

Ida Kate sat back, abashed. She wasn't usually so talkative—it must be the excitement of the day. She resolved to be the best hostess to Caroline. *You'll help me, won't you, Mama? After all, we want Caroline to be happy here.*

But Caroline was shaking her head. "You'll find that I don't scare very easily." Ida Kate smiled at the look that passed between her father and his intended bride.

At last they were turning in at the entrance to their property. Old Hickory, their shaggy black and white sheepdog, raced in circles around the wagon, barking his greeting. Ida Kate was eager to show Caroline around. She led Caroline into the sod house, pointing out that although it was fairly dark inside due to the thick sod walls and the low ceilings, they did have more light than many other homesteaders, because when Papa framed in the sod walls with wood just before Mama died, he'd also cut three *more* windows into the side walls. And all four windows had glass—something many homesteaders did without, covering the window openings with oilcloth or paper instead. Caroline nodded and made little murmurs of approval, but Ida Kate wondered how she really felt. She must have been used to much grander places, growing up in a wealthy North Carolina family.

The main room of the Demings' home had a large stove set into the wall between the two windows. When they'd first moved to the prairie, Mama had cooked the family's meals in pots suspended over an open fire outdoors. After their first successful crop, though, Papa had ordered a big black iron stove, and it had arrived on the train. The stove did a fine job of cooking their meals and warming the house as well. There were three small rooms leading off the main room: two bedrooms and a windowless storeroom. Ida Kate had turned her bedroom over to Caroline Fairchild and little Hanky. She would be sleeping in the storeroom until her father and Caroline married.

Papa dragged the heavy trunk into Caroline's bedroom and set it on the floor by the bed. Ida Kate looked around the room, trying to see it through Caroline's eyes. It was a pleasant room, with wide plank floorboards and one small window. The walls had been freshly whitewashed last year and gleamed now in the late-afternoon light. Ida Kate had picked some early cornflowers and put them into a jar of water on the windowsill. The simple spool bed was covered with Mama's best quilt—hearts, flowers, and birds in soft shades of blue on a white background. The baby was to sleep in Ida Kate's own baby bed, a crib with intricately carved, slatted sides that had been in the Deming family for generations already and had come with them to Kansas from Philadelphia.

Caroline set the baby down in the crib with relief. "Whew," she said. "Nap time, little one." She rubbed her arms and smiled at Ida Kate and Papa. "For one so little, he surely is a heavy lad!" But baby Hanky didn't want to take a nap. He sat up in the crib and raised his arms.

"Mama?" he cried. "Mama?"

"He's probably hungry," said Papa. "Ida Kate has a pot of stew ready. Would you like her to feed him while I show you the barn and the rest of the property?"

"Oh, yes," Caroline said quickly. "That is, if Ida Kate doesn't mind!"

"I don't mind trying," said Ida Kate. She held her arms out to Hanky. "Come on, Hanky. Do you like rabbit stew?"

He clung to her like a little monkey, and she carried him back to the main room, where the kettle of stew was keeping warm inside the black oven. While her father took Caroline out to see the barn and animals, the out-house, and the fields—just planted with the hardy new strain of wheat called Turkey Red that Papa hoped would turn them a fine profit—Ida Kate set the baby on her lap and mashed up some carrots and potatoes with gravy. She tried to feed Hanky small bites on the little silver spoon that had been her own baby spoon, but he pre-ferred to grab the mash with his hands and smear it into his mouth. It was messy, but fast.

"Can you talk?" she asked him. "Are you going to like having me for your big sister?"

"Mama?" asked the baby.

"She'll be along soon," Ida Kate told him—and then came the sound of hoofbeats outside, and laughing voices. Ida Kate hoisted the baby onto her hip and went to the door.

Two riders on horseback had entered their yard. Papa and Caroline were just walking back from the barn. "Greetings!" called William Ruppenthal, their neighbor from the next claim over, dismounting with a flourish. His daughter Martha grinned at Ida Kate from astride her dappled horse. In front of her she held a wicker basket covered by a white cloth.

"We couldn't wait to meet your guests," Martha called to Ida Kate.

Martha's fair braids were tied back with a big blue bow, and she was wearing her best Sunday dress, even though this was Thursday. She handed down the basket to Ida Kate, who had to take it with one hand since she was still holding Hanky with the other. Then Martha slid off her horse and tethered his reins to the fence. "So, tell me everything," she whispered to Ida Kate. "What's she like? Is she as nice as her letters? Can I hold the baby?"

Ida Kate passed Hanky to her friend. Martha was always talking a mile a minute, always eager for news or gossip. She was always the first to raise her hand at school, even though it was Ida Kate who more often had the correct answer. Martha was always coming up with games and projects, though it fell to Ida Kate to clean up afterward. The girls were a happy pair, with Martha usually the leader and Ida Kate the follower. The long prairie winters would seem much longer, Ida Kate suspected, if she didn't have Martha to play with. She would be so pleased to go back to school and see her friend more often, now that Caroline was here.

"We know you must be tired from your journey, and we don't mean to stay," said Mr. Ruppenthal after Papa introduced Caroline, "but my wife wanted me to bring you some bread and jam, and one of her dried-apple pies.

She plans to come in person to welcome you soon."

"Why, thank you kindly," said Caroline with a friendly
smile. "How delightful to have such good neighbors just
down the road."

Martha whispered to Ida Kate, "She surely is pretty.
But I thought you said she was tall with red hair!"

"Auburn—at least that's what she wrote. Maybe her
hair takes on red highlights in the summer sun."

"Well, at least the baby has red hair! He's a lovely
little lad."

The girls stood near the horses with the baby while
the adults talked in cheerful voices.

"This is the man I have to thank for the idea of writing
to the newspapers in search of a bride," Papa was telling
Caroline. "He had such good luck himself that way, I
thought I would try my own luck."

"And looks like your own luck runs pretty strong,"
said Mr. Ruppenthal. "Because here she is, and with a fine
boy, too, to be a son to you, Henry. Couldn't ask for more,
now could you?"

"No," said Ida Kate's father in his quiet, deep voice.
"We're just hoping she'll be happy here." He rested his
gaze on Caroline.

"Well, we won't keep you now," said Mr. Ruppenthal,
mounting his horse. "Ma'am, please accept our heartiest
wishes for your happiness here. We'll be seeing you
again soon."

"Are you coming to school tomorrow?" asked Martha, handing the baby back to Ida Kate and untying her horse's reins. She stepped up on the rung of the fence, then threw her leg over her horse.

"Not till Monday. I'll help Caroline settle in first," said Ida Kate.

"Then—good-bye, housework! Hello, lessons!" laughed Martha. "I hope you think it's a fair trade."

"I know it is," said Ida Kate earnestly. "You know I've missed school."

"Even Miss Butler?" Martha raised her eyebrows and pursed her lips in a parody of the schoolmistress's usual expression.

Ida Kate smiled. "Even Miss Butler!"

Martha waved and trotted off after her father, and then Ida Kate carried Hanky into the house.

"Mama?" asked the baby, looking all around him.

"Mrs. Fairchild—I mean, Caroline—I think he wants you," said Ida Kate.

"Oh—yes, of course. Come here, my lamb. Are you thirsty?" When Caroline took the baby, he patted the front of her dress in a gesture Ida Kate recognized. Martha's baby sister patted Mrs. Ruppenthal's dress in the same way when she was ready to nurse. But Caroline looked over at Ida Kate. "Do you have some fresh milk I can give him?"

"Yes," Ida Kate said, rather perplexed, and went to the pail of milk in the storeroom. She used the dipper to fill a cup for the baby.

Hanky slurped the milk eagerly while Caroline held him in her lap in the big rocking chair. Papa poked up the fire in the stove, and the two of them sat chatting together quietly while Ida Kate ladled out the stew for supper.

Darkness was falling outside—the early dusk of spring—and the evening was growing colder. Caroline trimmed the wick of the kerosene lamp on the sideboard and then lit it. It cast a warm glow around the room. She lit another lamp and set it on the shelf near the stove, then stooped to build up the fire in the oven. The flames sputtered and sent out a shower of sparks that flickered like little stars. Ida Kate looked around the room and thought how peaceful the scene was. It felt right having Caroline there. *Doesn't it, Mama?* She believed Mama agreed.

They sat at the table together, just as if they were already a family. Ida Kate served the stew, and Papa cut the bread. Hanky gnawed on a crust while everyone else ate. Caroline exclaimed over how delicious the meal was. "You're a fine cook, my girl," she said. "Your mother taught you well."

"Yes, she did," Ida Kate replied, "but I know how to make only a few dishes."

"Well, I'll be happy to take over as head cook from now on, Ida Kate," Caroline said, "if you'd like some help."

"Thank you, ma'am," said Ida Kate.

"Now, you two can cook together," said Papa. "As I

recall from your letters, Caroline, you haven't much experience with cookery. Your servants did that sort of work when you were a girl."

"Oh—of course," said Caroline. "But even though I'm not all that good at cooking, I do enjoy turning my hand to it. One learns by doing, isn't that right? Look how well Ida Kate has learned, simply by having to do the job."

After the meal had ended, Ida Kate served Margaretha Ruppenthal's delicious dried-apple pie. The fire in the stove crackled. Hanky dozed on Papa's lap as if he'd already claimed Ida Kate's father for his own. Caroline sat eating her pie with a dreamy expression on her face.

And then Ida Kate's little tabby kitten, Millie, jumped into Caroline's lap. Caroline reached out her hand and stroked her. The kitten mewed. She turned around three times before settling down onto Caroline's knee, purring.

"Gracious, I'm sorry!" said Ida Kate, putting down her fork and reaching for the kitten. "I've told her she's got to stay outdoors now that you're here."

"Whatever for?" asked Caroline, her hand still stroking the kitten's back. "She's a dear little thing."

"But cats make you sneeze—"

"Oh?" Caroline blinked. "Indeed they do, *usually*. But this little one doesn't seem to be having that effect on me. Could it be that Kansas kittens are different? Let's let her stay and see how we get on. If I start sneezing, out to the barn she'll go."

This suited Ida Kate very well. But there was a strange little tickle in the back of her mind as she watched her soon-to-be stepmother cuddle the kitten. A tickle that was trying to tell her something—but she brushed it firmly away.

CHAPTER 3
SNOOP!

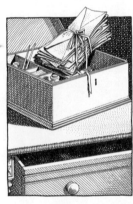 In the morning Ida Kate awoke to birdsong. She lay in bed, eyes closed, listening. She was trying to remember her dream—something about baking bread with Mama—when she realized she really was smelling the warm, yeasty fragrance of fresh bread. Her eyes popped open.

The bride! Caroline!

Ida Kate had meant to get up even earlier than usual to show their special visitor where all the baking supplies and crockery were kept, and how to make porridge and eggs for breakfast. She shoved back her quilt now and jumped out of the narrow bed. The storeroom was nearly dark, but light showed between the cracks in the plank door. Still in her nightdress, she opened the storeroom door and peeked into the big room. There was Caroline Fairchild, sliding loaves of hot bread out of the oven. She seemed to be coping just fine on her own. A pot of mush was warming on the stove top, and slices of meat were already set out on the table. Caroline must have been up before dawn to have prepared this breakfast. There was no sign of baby Hanky yet; he must still be asleep. No sign of Papa either, but he usually left early for the fields.

"Good morning, dear," Caroline said brightly, catching sight of Ida Kate in the doorway. "I thought you might like to sleep in for once. Your papa said you wouldn't be returning to school until Monday. And now that I'm here, you won't need to be up at the crack of dawn anymore. After all, a growing girl needs her rest."

Ida Kate stammered her thanks and ducked back into the dim storeroom. She felt flustered, unsure what to do. Since Mama had died, the cooking and baking had been her responsibility. She felt embarrassed and pleased at the same time to have this bride turn out to be so accomplished. It was a relief to have someone else take some of the burden from her. But, of course, that had been Papa's intention when he first wrote to the eastern newspapers advertising for a bride.

Ida Kate had helped him compose the piece. Every word of that letter was etched into her memory; they had both struggled hard to get the wording just right:

*GOOD WOMAN WANTED. Widowed Gentleman,
38 years, with Daughter of 12, seeks a Kind Lady of*

good heart and even temperament to travel to Kansas.
We make our home on 160 acres of prairie land, six miles
from the growing city of Hays. Object: Matrimony.

The letter to the newspapers resulted in five responses.
The first was from a widowed lady in Pennsylvania with
six sons, two daughters, and an old grandmother. She
wanted to know how big the house in Kansas was, and
how many servants there were. Papa had frowned at that
one. "Only four rooms," he had said, "and one serving girl
who needs to return to school!" The second was from a
girl in New York City, not much older than Ida Kate,
who wrote that she was bored with society and longing
for adventure. The third and fourth were from spinster
sisters in Boston, both older than Papa's own mother.
They wrote that he would be welcome to choose one of
them and that the other would come along to help out
in the house. And they hoped he would not mind building
an aviary for all their pet songbirds—seventeen in total.
Papa had laughed over that letter and asked Ida Kate
which one she'd prefer for a stepmother—Josephine or
Etta—and would she mind if they turned her bedroom
into the aviary?

But he'd been joking. He had replied politely to all
the letters, thanking the ladies for writing but saying that
his plans had changed. Then he tossed the letters into the
fire and sighed.

And then the fifth letter had arrived, and that was the one that thrilled them both. Ida Kate read it over and over. "This is the one," she told Papa. "I don't care who writes next! *This* is the lady for us. I just have a good feeling about her."

10th November 1877

Dear Sir,

My name is Caroline Fairchild, and I am writing in response to your advertisement.

I am a widow from North Carolina, where I grew up the daughter of a planter. Alas, my circumstances changed for the worse during the War, and now I live in Lynn, Massachusetts, where I work in Sorenson's Shoe and Boot Factory. It is employment which I hope very much to leave soon. I am interested in learning more about you and your daughter, and would hope also to learn more about your home in Kansas. I had never traveled far from North Carolina until moving north to Massachusetts last year, and I confess to being somewhat ignorant about the western territories and states. I imagine mountains and deserts and many buffalo!

Since the death of my husband, Clivedon Fairchild, over a year ago, I have lived a lonesome and desolate life, trying to care for our little son born six months after the death of his father. It saddens me that my son

*has never known a father's care and companionship.
In you, perhaps, he and I will both find what we
so sorely miss. Likewise, your daughter may know
once again a mother's love. I should very much enjoy
having a daughter.*

*I look forward to your response and remain
yours truly,*

Mrs. Caroline Fairchild

"I suppose she was a wealthy southern belle once,"
Papa had mused, reading the letter again, "whose family
lost their fortune. It's a fairly common story, I'm sure.
And circumstances forced her to move north and look for
work in the factory towns. Poor thing—I hear such work
is grueling. And she's widowed, with a baby! Now that's
hardship, Ida Kate. I think we might prove to be as much
a godsend for her as she will prove for us. Let us write
back to this lady and let her get to know us. We must take
things slowly—we don't want to rush her . . . but it could
be I've found my bride!"

Henry Deming had entered into a lively correspondence with Caroline Fairchild. He would ride into Hays
City each week to meet the train, and more often than
not there was a letter. Then he and Ida Kate would sit
at the table in the evening, reading and rereading.
Caroline Fairchild's letters made the long prairie winter
seem shorter. Papa and Ida Kate were learning a lot about

Caroline—and soon she felt like a familiar friend. She
and Papa shared a love of music—though neither could
carry a tune. Both came from wealthy families (although
Papa was quick to point out that his father had opposed
the move to Kansas and threatened to disinherit him),
and both desired a good education for their children.
Papa wrote: *I need the companionship of a good woman who
will take charge of our home. It is built of sod and wood—not
fancy, but strong—and has four rooms. I would be honored to
have you and your son call it your own.*

    Caroline wrote back, fretting that they would not find
her a very accomplished cook: *We had servants in the house
while I was growing up,* she wrote, *so I never had to learn
cooking or housekeeping until after the War, but then there was
not much money for anything fancy. I hope you will be patient,
for I am willing to do my best. I am a hard worker and a loving
mother, and I would rather be working for my own home and
family than for the factory owners. It will be quieter on the
prairie than in the factory, too, I daresay!*

    Papa replied, promising to be patient. He revealed a
weakness of his own: in inclement weather his war wound
sometimes caused him to limp. *But it doesn't keep me from
dancing at the Grand Ball at nearby Fort Hays, the highlight
of our social season!* he wrote.

    Once it was clear that Caroline would come to them,
Ida Kate wrote a letter too:

1st February 1878

Dear Mrs. Fairchild,

We are so happy. We got your letter saying you are really coming to us. Papa has read it a dozen times, always with a big smile. I am glad you have a baby. My mama's babies died, and the doctor said she mustn't have more. But she died anyway two winters ago of a foul sickness, nothing to do with babies.

But my own health is good, and so is Papa's. When you come to us in the spring, our garden will just be start-ing to grow. Sunflowers grow wild all over the prairie, but I like to plant them in our vegetable garden, too. Don't worry about the housework and cooking, because I am used to doing it, and I will help you. When I am not at school. We will come to meet you at the depot. Soon! Soon!

Please accept my good wishes for a safe journey for you and your baby.

Yours very truly,
Ida Kate Deming

P.S. There are no more buffalo in Kansas. But the prairie is home to prairie dogs, jackrabbits, coyote, deer, rattlesnakes, badgers, and antelope. There are bluegills, bass, and catfish in Big Creek, some miles from our home. And meadowlarks sing outside my window every morning.

Now Ida Kate poured water from the jug into the big bowl on the storeroom table. After she washed, she slipped on her everyday calico that she wore for housework and stepped out of the storeroom, hairbrush and ribbons in hand. There was a small mirror on the shelf by the stove. Ida Kate stood before it to tame her tangles.

"Here, dear, let me braid your hair for you." Caroline laid down the knife she'd been using to slice thick slabs of the hot bread. "Give me the hairbrush."

Since Mama's death, Ida Kate had gotten used to struggling with her own long hair, trying to get the part straight and all the wisps captured neatly. Papa sometimes tried to help, but he was hopeless. She smiled at Caroline now and handed her the brush—and Caroline had Ida Kate's shiny brown hair neatly braided in less than a minute! Caroline tied the ends of the two thick braids with the faded yellow ribbons and gave them a tug.

"There you go," she said. "But I do think some new ribbons are in order." She rummaged in the reticule she'd left in the corner and handed Ida Kate a small paper packet. "Here you go, dear. A friend from my boardinghouse makes ribbons all day. She gave me some for you."

"Thank you kindly!" Ida Kate sat at the table and tore open the packet, exclaiming over the assortment of ribbons—pink striped, yellow, cornflower blue, and white satin. "These are the most beautiful I've ever had!"

Millie leaped up onto the table to bat at them, but Ida Kate gently pushed her away.

"Let's put the blue ones in your hair today to match your dress," said Caroline. "And save the old ones for Millie. But now eat your breakfast while I finish washing up the dishes—"

A cry from Caroline's bedroom interrupted her. "Oh— the baby!" she exclaimed.

"May *I* go to him?" Ida Kate asked, her mouth still full of warm bread.

"Yes indeed," replied Caroline.

Ida Kate hurried into the bedroom. It looked so different with Caroline's belongings spread about and Hanky chortling at her from the crib. He held his arms out.

"Mama?" he asked.

"Your mama is washing dishes," Ida Kate told him, lifting him over the bars. "My oh my, you're soaking wet, poor little one." She had very little experience with babies. "Let's go find your mama."

"Oh, dear," moaned Caroline when she saw Hanky. "What a messy little fellow you've turned out to be. Well, I suppose we must wash you . . . Ida Kate, be a dear and put some water on the stove to heat for his bath. And we must soak these garments . . ."

Ida Kate stripped the wet clothing off the baby and wrapped him in one of Papa's flannel shirts. She held him and fed him egg and mush while the water heated for his bath. He was a soft, warm bundle in her lap, and she nuzzled the back of his neck, thinking of the two tiny babies—one a sister, one a brother—that had lived only a few days each. If only they'd lived . . . If only Mama had lived . . .

But then she pushed those thoughts away. Caroline and Hanky were here now, and they were going to be a family! *You're glad too, aren't you, Mama?*

And she felt the answer throb in the air: *Oh, yes, my darling.*

Ida Kate and Caroline worked at home together all morning, tending to the baby and preparing a vegetable pie for the midday meal. Ida Kate showed Caroline where all the dishes and cutlery were kept, how the pump outside worked to draw fresh, cold water, and what she'd planted out in the vegetable garden.

"You're a very accomplished housekeeper," Caroline told Ida Kate, looking over the fresh green shoots in the garden. "You seem to have things well in hand here—all by yourself."

"Well, Mama taught me to help because she was very frail," replied Ida Kate.

"You must miss your mama," Caroline said, her blue eyes meeting Ida Kate's gray ones.

"Oh, yes, I do," said Ida Kate. "But she's an angel now, and I think she's still with me. I . . . I sense her sometimes, I really do. Like a nice, loving presence. I believe Mama can see every single thing that happens here. I feel quite sure she's watching over us right now."

"Oh, my," said Caroline, sounding a bit startled. "Indeed!"

The day was fresh and warm, still springlike, and Ida Kate hoped it really *was* spring—not the false spring her father had predicted. It made Ida Kate want to ride over to Martha's and visit—but, of course, Martha would be in school this morning. *Soon! Soon!* sang Ida Kate to herself. She would go back next week.

The morning was so warm that Caroline decided to wash her dusty traveling clothes and Hanky's soiled flannel diapers, even though wash day was usually Monday. Ida Kate lugged the heavy iron kettle out of the storeroom and set it over the circle of stones in the yard. Caroline built the fire while Ida Kate carried buckets of water from the pump to fill the kettle, water sloshing out at her feet as the heavy pails bumped against her thighs. Together she and Caroline lifted and tipped the buckets to pour the water into the kettle. Together they sorted the clothing into whites and colors while the water heated. Then they took turns stirring the boiling brew of soft soap, water, and clothing in the huge vat. Laundry day was usually Ida Kate's very worst day—with the fire either burning too hot or going out altogether, with ash blowing all over the yard in the wind and dirtying the clean clothes—but the job wasn't nearly so terrible with two people working together. Ida Kate had forgotten.

At midday Papa came in from the fields, grinning to see Ida Kate and Hanky playing with the kitten on the front step and Caroline pegging the last of the baby's diapers onto the clothesline. She greeted him with a welcoming smile. He hugged Ida Kate and swept the baby up in the air.

"This is what I've been missing," he said to Caroline as they all went inside the house. "Wife and children waiting with the meal on the table—and Ida Kate outdoors *playing*!" He shook his head, setting Hanky down again. "You don't know how it has pained me to come home and see my little daughter toiling over her chores, with never a moment to play."

"All children need time to play," agreed Caroline. "Big and little ones alike."

"Adults, too," said Papa, and a look passed between them—a look that seemed full of words. Caroline smiled gently and put her hand on his arm. "I think we've both been through some very hard times, Henry," she murmured. "But I like to think they're over now . . . and that there will be time to play. For all of us."

He stared down at her hand on his arm, then slowly clasped it with his other hand. Her hand was so much smaller, his covered it completely. They didn't say anything at all, but Ida Kate, watching, felt a current of

understanding pulse between them. It made her feel
warm inside.

They sat at the table and ate the vegetable pie and
stewed apples, laughing and talking together as if they had
known each other longer than only a day. Caroline enter-
tained them with hilarious tales of her fellow passengers
on the long train journey—the woman who had traveled
as far as St. Louis with a noisy green parrot on her shoulder,
and the man with a gray beard so long it practically needed
a seat of its own. Her hearty laughter was loud and infec-
tious, and Ida Kate, giggling, decided Caroline must not
have been a very proper southern belle after all.

After the meal it was time for Hanky's nap. "Would
you give the baby his milk first, then put him to bed, Ida
Kate?" asked Caroline as Papa clapped on his hat and prepared to return to the fields for the afternoon. "I would
like to walk out with your father for a short time."

"Well, I'll try," said Ida Kate agreeably, and Papa laid
his big hand on his daughter's head for a moment before
stepping out the door with Caroline. Ida Kate watched
from the window as the two of them headed out the gate
and toward the barn. They looked so natural side by side,
as if they belonged together. Ida Kate had not seen her
father with many women other than Mama, although in
the two years since Mama's death, all the single women
in the area had presented themselves to him at one time
or another: the two elderly seamstresses in Hays City

who confessed to Papa one day at the general store that
they found him a sinfully handsome man; Jennie Tate,
the daughter of the saddlemaker, urged by her worried
father to marry instead of running off to New York to
try her luck as an opera singer; and then, of course,
Miss Artemia Butler, the schoolmarm.

Thank goodness none of these ladies had won Papa's
heart!

Ida Kate went over to pour a dipperful of milk from
the pail into Hanky's cup. Then she carried the baby into
her bedroom and changed his wet garments. Caroline
had pinned the diaper so loosely, Ida Kate saw, it was
no wonder the poor lad was soaking. She folded a clean
diaper and fastened it securely, the way she had seen
Martha diaper the Ruppenthal baby, then settled into
the rocking chair with Hanky on her lap. He snuggled
against her, his soft red curls tickling her chin as she
bent over him. She hummed as she rocked, liking the
sweet weight of him against her. She closed her eyes
and almost hummed herself to sleep right along with
Hanky—until she felt a hand on her shoulder. Her eyes
flew open.

"I'll take him now," Caroline whispered, and lifted
Hanky into her arms. "Seems you have the magic touch."

Ida Kate smiled. "I wasn't sure I could get him to
sleep, but he nodded right off," she said, pleased with
Caroline's praise.

"I think he's happy to be away from the boarding-house," Caroline murmured. "He had to stay with a baby minder all day while . . . while I worked in the factory." Her face clouded. "I know I'm glad to be away, myself."

She tucked Hanky into the crib. Then she and Ida Kate tiptoed out of the room.

They spent the rest of the afternoon together, doing the chores in the house and in the barn. Ida Kate had thought she would need to show Caroline how to take care of the animals, because wealthy southern belles couldn't be expected to know how to feed the pigs or curry the horses or milk the cows. But Caroline made friends with the animals quickly and seemed to know just what to do. They got the work done in half the usual time, and Ida Kate glowed with the happy feeling that life was going to be easier now that Caroline had come. As the sun began to set, Ida Kate brought in the laundry from the line, folding it loosely as she placed it in the wicker baskets. No doubt the next day's ironing would be easier, too, with Caroline to help. One of them could heat some of the irons while the other pressed wrinkles out of the garments. On her own, Ida Kate lost a lot of time because she had to heat and carry the irons all by herself.

Lugging the wicker baskets inside, she found Caroline at the stove, stirring a pot of fragrant soup and singing as she worked. Her voice was lovely! Ida Kate listened with pleasure from the doorway, thinking how homey the house felt with someone else inside during the long after-noon before Papa came in from work.

"You sing like an angel," Ida Kate said when Caroline turned and saw her. "I don't know why you wrote that you couldn't keep a tune—you have a perfect voice! I think you're far too modest!"

A flush started up Caroline's neck, and she turned back to her soup pot. "I do like to sing," she replied. "But I surely wouldn't say I'm especially tuneful, and I'm cer-tainly far from . . . angelic." She set a bowl of potatoes on the table and handed Ida Kate the paring knife.

Ida Kate peeled the potatoes, diced them, and added them to the pot of soup. Then she looked up to ask Caroline what else she'd like done—but Caroline had left the room. She must have gone to check on Hanky. The soup was bubbling, the bread was sliced; everything was nearly ready for their meal. Ida Kate drew in a happy breath and headed for Papa's room. One of her favorite things to do when she had free time was to look through Mama's books on the shelf next to the big double bed. But she hadn't had free time in a long while.

Mama had been a schoolteacher back in Philadelphia before she'd married Papa, and she was an avid reader.

Even when she was very weak from her illness, she would pat the bed and invite Ida Kate to sit with her. Then Mama would read aloud from her books. Stories from the Bible. Stories of adventure—like tales of King Arthur and his knights of the Round Table, or Harriet Beecher Stowe's *Uncle Tom's Cabin.* And poetry. Ida Kate's favorite poem had been Whittier's "Snow-Bound"—until Mama died during the snowstorm. She and Mama had been able to recite the opening verses together. Last spring Papa had bought Mark Twain's new *Adventures of Tom Sawyer* for Ida Kate, but it still sat unread on Mama's little shelf. Maybe there would be time for reading again, now that Caroline had arrived.

Ida Kate lifted the latch of Papa's bedroom door and swung it open. "Oh!" she cried out in surprise.

Caroline Fairchild turned with a start. She was standing in front of Papa's dresser, and in her hands she held the packet of letters she'd sent to Papa over the months of their correspondence. "Oh!" she echoed Ida Kate. "I was just . . . dusting in here, and I found these letters. How sweet that Henry has kept them all."

"Well, of course he would keep them!" said Ida Kate with a smile, coming into the room. "We both read them over and over during the winter. We couldn't wait for you to arrive. And now you're really here!"

"Yes, now I'm really here," murmured Caroline. She retied the letters with the faded ribbon and replaced the packet in the wooden box atop the dresser. She closed the lid.

"I should get back to work," she said, picking up her dust cloth.

"The room surely mustn't be too dusty," Ida Kate told her earnestly. "I mean, I cleaned the house very carefully so it would be ready for you . . ."

"Oh, no, it looks very nice," Caroline said. "Everything is really quite . . . quite perfect." She smiled faintly, then turned and left the room.

Ida Kate stared after her, troubled, as a thought flickered in her mind before she hurriedly extinguished it: Had Caroline really been cleaning—or had she been *snooping?*

CHAPTER 4

A KILLING
AT CASTLE ROCK

The next day was Saturday. Papa suggested that as a special treat they hurry with the morning chores, then pack a picnic lunch and drive out to Castle Rock. "You simply must see the Rock," he told Caroline over a breakfast of hotcakes and sweet butter.

Castle Rock was a tremendous out-cropping of rock some distance from Hays City, towering up over the prairie—the tallest point for miles around. It rose like a huge stone fortress, and whenever Ida Kate approached it, she felt as if she were arriving at King Arthur's ancient castle, with all the knights of the Round Table and their ladies waiting for her inside, and Merlin the Magician, too, casting secret spells.

Since Mama died there hadn't been any picnics at all, at least not with Papa. Ida Kate had joined the Ruppenthals for outings on more than one occasion, but the magic wasn't there anymore.

A picnic today with Caroline and Hanky would be fun, she decided. And she helped Caroline prepare the lunch they would take. They packed a loaf of warm bread, ham sliced for sandwiches, a tub of fresh butter, fresh eggs gathered and boiled just that morning, a brick of cheese, and, to top it all off, a jam cake with raisins that Caroline had baked the day before.

It certainly seemed things were going more smoothly now that Caroline was finally here. Already Ida Kate felt more rested than she used to. She didn't have to wake as early; she didn't have to spend as much time on house-work. Caroline had things well in hand. Pretty good going, Ida Kate thought appreciatively, for a once-pampered southern belle!

She darted an affectionate look at Caroline as Papa helped his mail-order bride up onto the high seat of the wagon. He lifted Hanky into the back with Ida Kate, and the two of them settled into a nest of old horse blankets. Papa stowed his Winchester rifle, which usually hung over the front door, safely beneath the buckboard seat. Last of all he lifted the picnic hamper into the back of the wagon. "Guard this with your very lives," he told the children solemnly. Hanky laughed and reached up to pull Papa's beard, and Ida Kate giggled.

"We will fend off all invaders, my liege," she vowed, lifting her arm as if she were wielding an imaginary sword.

They left Old Hickory behind to guard the farm and

set off down the rutted track across the prairie toward
Hays City. Then they took the fork that led across the
miles to Castle Rock. The day was fine and sunny, and the
chirps and twitters of birds in the prairie grasses blended
in a fine symphony of sound as the wagon passed by. After
a while Caroline started singing along with the birds. Her
voice was a pleasure to hear, and it blew with the wind
back to Ida Kate and Hanky.

*Hear that, Mama? Isn't that the loveliest music you ever did
hear?* Ida Kate felt her mama's answer blow through her:
Mama was happy about Caroline, happy that Ida Kate had
someone to help her in the house now, and happy that
Papa wasn't lonely anymore.

Hanky pressed against Ida Kate's side as they traveled.
He chuckled and patted his hands together and tried to
open the picnic basket. She lifted the lid and tore off a
small hunk of bread for him. She liked this baby. She
wished he could talk, though. Babies would probably have
a lot to say, she reflected, if only they knew the words.
What adventures had Hanky already had in his young life?
What had it been like living in a factory town? What had
he seen on his train journey across the country?

"You'll tell me someday," she murmured against his
silky red curls.

"Mama!" he chortled. It seemed to be his only word.

Finally they arrived at Castle Rock. Caroline looked
duly impressed. "Amazing," she said. "You almost expect

to see a moat and turrets and flags waving, don't you?"

"Exactly," said Papa, swinging her down from the wagon. "It's our very own local palace—chief residence of His Majesty, the King of Kansas."

"And his queen, I hope?" asked Caroline, slanting a teasing glance up at him.

"And his queen, of course," he said, smiling. "The story wouldn't be complete without the queen." He paused and raised a hand to brush back a lock of golden brown hair that had escaped from Caroline's bonnet. "No story would be."

Ida Kate hugged Hanky. Things were working out so well for all of them!

They clambered on the rocks, Papa carrying the baby on his shoulders. They explored all around Castle Rock. No other visitors were there that morning, and Ida Kate played that she was Merlin. She commanded Hanky to lift King Arthur's magical sword from the stone. Instead, he picked up a pebble and toddled over to hand it to her. "Yes!" she cried, bowing low. "You have done it! You have proved yourself to be the true king. Camelot shall be yours!" Hanky stared up at her, eyes wide. Caroline and Papa—as queen and king—bowed to him.

Still laughing, they set out their royal feast on the cloth that Caroline spread across the ground. They devoured everything, leaving only crumbs from the jam cake for the prairie dogs that poked their heads up from their holes and peeked out at them. When the sun had moved past midday and Hanky was drooping over his cup of milk, Papa said it was time to return home. The animals were waiting, and there were still chores to be done.

Ida Kate was pleased the picnic had lasted so long. Most often since Mama died, Papa just buried himself in work, never stopping long enough for fun. Another welcome change now that Caroline was here.

Caroline and Papa folded the picnic cloth. "Please go get the baby now, Ida Kate," said Papa, and she set off for Hanky, who, too tired to toddle, had crawled over to a nearby outcropping of rock and was sitting there, sifting little stones through his fingers. Ida Kate reached down to fetch him—then stopped in alarm.

She stood statue-still. She didn't dare to breathe. There—right there, just inches from Hanky—was a large, coiled rattlesnake.

The rattlesnake's tail twitched; Ida Kate heard the warning, the ominous rattle that meant the snake was ready to strike. "Papa . . . ?" Her voice was only the merest breath of a whisper, but Papa, coming up right behind her, was quick. His foot, covered with a thick leather boot, darted out and caught the snake just behind the head, pinning it down hard on the ground. Fast as lightning, Ida Kate snatched Hanky into her arms and backed away. The snake whipped its body from side to side, thrashing its tail wildly.

"Caroline!" bellowed Papa. "Quick, fetch me the rifle—no, the axe! From the wagon!"

Ida Kate was holding Hanky so tightly he started to howl. She felt like screaming herself, but she held her breath instead. The snake lashed back and forth, trying to strike her papa. Rattlesnake bites were fatal; many a Kansas settler died of snakebite. The snake had to be killed, and Papa knew the surest way to do it.

"The axe!" he shouted. "Hurry!"

And then there came Caroline, running toward him from the wagon. Papa, twisting out of the way of the thrashing snake, grabbed for the axe—"*Quick, woman, give it here!*"—but Caroline raised it over her head and slammed it down right next to Papa's boot, slicing clear through the snake's body and severing the head neatly with a single blow.

Papa stared at her in astonishment. He waited for the snake's thrashing to stop. When it did, he lifted his foot and stepped back. "Whoa!" he said. He shook his head at her in wonder. "Couldn't have done a better job myself."

Ida Kate was equally impressed. *Amazing!*

Caroline handed Papa the axe. She gathered Hanky into her arms. "That varmint can't hurt you now," she said.

Ida Kate saw the admiration in Papa's eyes as he looked at his mail-order bride. "No simpering southern belles around here, no sir!"

Caroline tossed her head and hugged Hanky. "Well, it was nothing. You think we don't have snakes down in South Carolina?"

They all laughed and headed for the wagon. Then Ida Kate stopped. "Wait—North Carolina, wasn't it, Caroline? Not South—*North!*"

Caroline stopped laughing. A sudden blush stained her cheeks. "*North* Carolina, of course," she said firmly. "That's what I said."

CHAPTER 5

STORM CLOUDS

O n Sunday mornings Ida Kate
would rise even earlier than usual
to collect the eggs and milk the cow.
While Papa tended to the pigs and
harnessed the horses to the wagon,
Ida Kate would hurriedly prepare a
basket to take along to church for the
potluck luncheon afterward—perhaps
baked beans she'd made the night before, or a plate of
cornbread. Then Papa and Ida Kate would wash and dress
in their best clothes, and they'd set off, eating a breakfast
of bread and cheese as they rode across the prairie to
church.

This first Sunday with their special guest was different.
Caroline was up even earlier than Ida Kate, gathering the
eggs and milking Bessie and Bonnie, and unpacking the
rest of the belongings from her trunk and reticule. A hot
breakfast was already cooked and waiting on the table
when Ida Kate awoke—a fine meal of bacon and eggs and

fried bread. When Papa came in from the barn, they all
ate together. Ida Kate's braids were fixed more neatly than
usual and tied back with a perky bow at the nape of her
neck, thanks to Caroline's attentions. And Hanky was
dressed in clean clothes, his red curls damp and shining.

They all climbed into the wagon and set off. Caroline
wore her blue serge traveling suit again, and the impractical little hat. She held the food she had prepared for the
luncheon: a large bowl of potato salad made with cooked
egg, crumbled bacon, onions, and cream. She looked
quite elegant sitting next to Papa on the high buckboard
seat, and Ida Kate felt a little thrill of pride in her pretty,
accomplished, soon-to-be stepmother.

Ida Kate sat with Hanky in the back of the wagon
as they had the day before, but this time they did not
cuddle together in the nest of blankets. She sat on a
wooden crate, with Hanky on her lap, trying to keep
both of their outfits neat as the wagon jolted along the
rutted path.

"How far is the church?" asked Caroline.

"All the way back into town," Papa replied. "We're holding services in the courthouse until our new Presbyterian
church is finished. A good stone building. It'll be ready for
us sometime next year, I expect."

Some church groups held services at the fort. The
Catholic settlers had erected a church last year. New
Russian immigrants had plans for an Orthodox church,

and the Lutherans hoped to start building their own soon as well. *There's room enough on the prairie for everybody's churches to be built,* thought Ida Kate as Papa tethered the horses outside the courthouse.

Inside they found seats together near the back, in case Hanky couldn't sit still and needed to be taken outside. There were more people than usual today, Ida Kate noticed. Those sitting on the front benches turned to look back at her family as they got settled. Everybody knew that Henry Clay Deming had sent east for a bride. Everybody wanted to see her. The pianist struck some dramatic chords, and the congregation stood to sing the opening hymn.

The pastor, Rupert Smiley, welcomed everyone. Ida Kate always had to hide a smile when she saw him because he was so completely unlike his name. He was tall and thin and always wore black suits, and he never, ever smiled. Ida Kate looked around as she listened to the sermon. William Ruppenthal, Martha's father, sat with his nine-year-old twin sons on the other side of the courthouse. The boys, Jimmy and Johnny, waved to Ida Kate. But where were Martha and her stepmother and the little ones?

Miss Butler was not at the church service this morning either. But Miss Butler's father and mother, the plump and comfortable elderly couple who owned the general store, were sitting across the aisle. They nodded over at

the Demings. Children Ida Kate knew from school sat
with their families. There were the Granger children, and
the Paulsen boys, and little Maisie Groninger. Ida Kate
would be seeing all of them at school the very next day—
and she couldn't wait!

Little Hanky sat on Caroline's lap and played with
Papa's pocket watch. He was really being very good,
Ida Kate thought. Better than some of the other babies,
who were sniveling or fussing.

Pastor Smiley was speaking about the need to be
hospitable to strangers, to be charitable and open, and
to invite others in—"for you do not know," he preached,
"when you are entertaining angels unaware." All very well
for *him* to say, thought Ida Kate wryly. The good pastor
was notorious for keeping to himself. He *never* enter-
tained, as far as she knew.

I'd know an angel if ever I saw one, wouldn't I, Mama?

"Jesus came and they did not know him," Pastor Smiley
intoned. "So take heed. Keep watch . . . for you know not
when the master of the house will come!" A gust of wind
rattled the window of the courthouse as if in emphasis.

After the sermon Ida Kate moved outdoors with the
others, behind the courthouse where the luncheon tables
were set up. The tables were covered with white cloths
and held huge quantities of food brought by the church-
goers. The tablecloths flapped in the breeze. Ida Kate got
in line and took a sturdy white plate from the stack of

china. She loaded her plate with a piece of chicken, some fresh bread, and Caroline's potato salad. Their mail-order bride had been entirely too modest, thought Ida Kate as she sat down at one of the long tables and took her first bite of creamy potato salad. It was delicious! *Imagine telling us she'd never really learned to cook!* Ida Kate shook her head. What utter nonsense.

People were crowding around Papa and Caroline now, wanting to be introduced. Ida Kate offered to take Hanky and feed him, and Caroline handed him over gratefully. Ida Kate and Hanky sat with Maisie Groninger and some of the other children from school, and Ida Kate fed Hanky bites of potato salad and chicken. She enjoyed showing off her almost-brother, and Hanky was most entertaining, putting his slice of bread on his head like a hat. They all chattered and laughed while the adults talked at the other tables. Ida Kate could hear Caroline's pleasant southern drawl mingling with the other voices. When Ida Kate finished her meal, she carried Hanky over to join Papa and Caroline.

"Yes, indeedy," Mr. Butler was saying as Ida Kate sat down on the bench next to Papa, "Artemia has been under the weather. I think it's this sudden warm spell we're having."

"I'm sorry Miss Butler is ill," Ida Kate spoke up politely. "I'm very eager to return to school tomorrow. Do you think she will be well enough to teach?"

The elderly shopkeeper cocked an eyebrow at Ida Kate. "I think so. She is very dedicated. Her mother and I prevailed upon her to rest today, but I expect she'll be up and ready for her duties tomorrow."

"I'm sure that she is pleased you are finally able to return, my dear," added Mrs. Butler kindly.

"Well, it's thanks to Caroline," said Ida Kate. She smiled across the table at her soon-to-be stepmother. "And I shall save her a front-row seat at our school recital."

"And what will you be reciting?" asked Caroline.

"An essay I started ages ago on Henry Clay, the famous abolitionist. I'll finally have a chance to finish and memorize it, now that you're here."

Papa refilled everyone's glasses of cider from the big pitcher and poured Ida Kate a glass, too. "I was named for old Henry Clay," he told the others. "As was my father. It was my father's greatest sadness that I did not have a son to pass the name along to."

Caroline reached over and tickled Hanky under his chin. "Maybe someday this fellow will want to change his name from Henry Claude to Henry Clay," she said, "even though he was named for his father."

Claude? A sudden chill pounced across Ida Kate's shoulders. *Claude Fairchild?*

"My father was also a staunch abolitionist," Mrs. Butler was saying now. "And a supporter of Abraham Lincoln.

I think it was the most tragic moment of my father's life when he heard that President Lincoln had been shot. He revered the man—felt he was truly one of the greats. No president has measured up since."

"That's what my father said, too," Caroline said eagerly. "He even saw Lincoln in person once—and was most favorably impressed."

"Now where did your father meet the president?" asked Mrs. Butler, leaning across the table toward Caroline. "My own father would have given his eyeteeth to have met the man!"

"It wasn't a personal meeting," Caroline told her. "But the president spoke at an abolitionist rally in New York, and my father and brother were there. They never forgot how impressive he looked, and how very tall . . ."

Caroline's voice trailed off as she caught Ida Kate staring at her in openmouthed surprise. And when she spoke again, her southern accent seemed more pronounced than before. "That was a long time ago, of course."

"Of course," said Mrs. Butler, a little frown appearing on her already-lined forehead. "But I am surprised to hear your father was an abolitionist! That must have been exceedingly unusual for a southern plantation owner."

"Indeed, it would have been!" her husband chimed in. "Tell us about your family, Mrs. Fairchild. Were they not slave owners?"

Caroline shifted uncomfortably. "Well . . . yes, they were," she admitted.

Then she stood up quickly and reached across the table to lift Hanky out of Papa's arms. "I think we'll have to be heading home now," she said. "The wind is rising, and Hanky is due for a nap."

"Oh, the other mothers with little ones just put their babies down to sleep in the courthouse," Mrs. Groninger informed her. "Tucked up snug on a bench."

But Caroline was shaking her head. "No, I think this little fellow has had so much upheaval lately, what with all the train travel and the new surroundings, he'll do better to sleep in one place for a while." Caroline's voice was smooth, but Ida Kate saw her eyes darting nervously. "Ready, Mr. Deming? Ready, Ida Kate?" She moved away from the table, carrying the baby, without waiting for their answer.

Papa stood up. He bowed to the women and shook hands with all the men at the table, then fetched the nearly empty bowl of potato salad from the buffet.

Ida Kate said polite good-byes to everybody, then slowly followed after Papa and Caroline. Ida Kate's head was pounding now with thoughts that made her feel slightly sick.

Later in the afternoon, while Hanky napped, the wind picked up and blew colder. Ida Kate shook the wire basket of corn over the fire and made a mountain of crisp, fresh popcorn. Papa mended a broken harness, poking into the leather with his sharp awl and threading a leather cord through the holes. Caroline brought out a green striped dress from her trunk and offered to alter it to fit Ida Kate. It would be a good school dress, she said.

So Ida Kate thanked her and tried the dress on and stood still while Caroline measured and tucked and pinned. Evening shadows began to fall as Caroline hemmed the green striped skirt. Hanky woke up, and Ida Kate showed him how to play with the little wooden Noah's ark that had always been her favorite Sunday toy. She marched the carved animals two by two up the ramp and let Hanky dump them inside the boat. She made the giraffes peek out the little windows at him. Hanky chuckled, Caroline smiled, Papa ate popcorn and gazed around the room at his family.

Everything looked cozy. Everything seemed so peaceful.

Papa looks so content, thought Ida Kate, and the observation filled her with despair. She stacked the little wooden animals in a pile for Hanky to knock over, then set them up again and again. Outside, the wind rattled the windowpanes and the sky grew dark. She felt that she and Papa and Hanky and Caroline were all sitting together inside one of the thick, impenetrable clouds that could sweep across the prairie without warning. A storm cloud.

Ida Kate shivered and let the unwelcome niggles in the back of her mind take shape. Everything *seemed* peaceful, yet something was not right.

Something was very wrong about Caroline.

CHAPTER 6

SCHOOL DAZE

Ida Kate hurried along the trail to school, anxious to talk to Martha. She had left home as early as she could, unable to eat the hot mush and fried egg that Caroline set before her. She needed to be away from the house, away from her growing dread. But the dread traveled with her as she walked the packed dirt trail.

I've got to talk to Martha, Ida Kate told herself. *Maybe she'll tell me I'm imagining things . . .*

But she knew she was not imagining things.

Old Hickory had wanted to trot along with her to school, but she'd ordered him to stay home to keep watch. He thumped his tail and waited at the fence.

The path that Ida Kate now walked stretched miles across the prairie toward Hays. The vast grassland had a life of its own and was never silent. As Ida Kate walked she heard clicks and whistles, rustlings and murmurings. These noises made some people nervous, but to Ida Kate they seemed a kind of music. Prairie music. The song comforted her now as she hurried along the rutted wagon track.

She stopped when she reached the Ruppenthals' sod house, one very much like Ida Kate's own house, but still in the process of being framed in with wood. Mr. Ruppenthal, high on a ladder propped against one wall, waved.

"I missed Martha at church," Ida Kate called up to him as she reached the house. "I do hope she is well enough to come to school today."

"Martha's just fine," he assured her. "It was little Davy and Edmund who were feeling poorly. So Margaretha and Martha stayed home with them and the baby." He climbed down from the ladder and led Ida Kate to the door of the little house. "Little fellas seem better now."

"I am very glad to hear it," said Ida Kate sincerely. All the settlers feared sickness. Every season brought its illnesses, and so often the doctor was not able to help. The graveyard at the edge of town increased in size every year, and after the last hard winter, some people joked that the cemetery was growing faster than Hays City itself. Fortunately this wasn't quite true. But Ida Kate was glad no one was ill now at the Ruppenthals' house.

All six Ruppenthal children were clustered around their large table in the small dark kitchen when Ida Kate poked her head in the door.

"You're nice and early," Mrs. Ruppenthal said in her

strong German accent as she buttered a wedge of bread
for Ida Kate. She was a plump woman with yellow braids
coiled around her head like a crown. "All right, Jimmy
and Johnny, don't forget your lunch pails. Martha, dearest,
you and Ida Kate see that they remember to bring them
home again!"

The way she pronounced it, "Martha" sounded like
Marta. She pronounced "Ida" *Eeda,* which always made
Ida Kate smile. But today Ida Kate couldn't smile. She
was desperate to talk to her friend alone.

"I wanna go, too," said Edmund, eyeing the older children wistfully as they left the house.

"Next year, lamb," Ida Kate heard his mother say
soothingly. "When you are old enough to walk the
whole way."

The schoolhouse was three miles from the Ruppenthals'
house. Ida Kate knew they were lucky to be so close.
The children who lived in Hays City attended school in
a fine new stone building, but the children who lived out
on the prairie attended the one-room sod schoolhouse,
and some had to travel many miles to get there.

"I'm so glad you're coming back to school," said Martha,
reaching over and squeezing Ida Kate's hand. "It's just
not been the same since you had to leave."

"I'm glad, too," Ida Kate said. "I've missed everyone,
even Miss Butler—can you believe it?" Then she lowered
her voice. "But, Martha, I'm dying to talk to you."

"Yes, you must tell me everything! What are they like together, your father and Mrs. Fairchild? Are they romantic?"

The twins made kissing noises at their side. Martha shoved them away. The boys had identical round blue eyes and identical crops of yellow hair that stuck up even when their stepmother wet it down. The twins seemed to have perpetually sticky fingers and moved in a whirlwind of noise and dust.

"Oh, marry me, my darling bride!" cooed Johnny—or was it Jimmy?

"Oh, my true love!" sighed the other twin. They fell into a fit of giggles.

"Oh, get out of here," groaned Martha. "Leave us in peace!"

"First one to the schoolhouse wins the pie in my lunch!" Ida Kate told them. Food was a great motivating force for Martha's twin brothers.

Jimmy and Johnny whooped with delight. In seconds they were off, hurtling down the path.

"That was inspired," said Martha. "I can see you'll make a fine big sister."

"You're moving things along too fast—Hanky's not even really my brother." Ida Kate swung her lunch pail in agitation.

"Not yet. But you already know that bribery is a big sister's most important trick." Martha laughed. "Bet it feels odd to have a baby in the house, doesn't it?" She was always avid for details, always as excited about other people's lives as she was about her own. "Having a baby brother's bound to feel strange since you're an only child, but soon it'll feel so *right* . . ."

Ida Kate watched the dust fly up behind the boys. They rounded a curve in the track ahead and then were out of sight. Ida Kate took a deep breath. "Martha, there's something so *wrong*."

"Wrong? With Hanky?"

"With Caroline Fairchild." Somehow Ida Kate felt like a traitor saying even this much.

Martha looked intrigued. "Uh-oh, no romance after all? Your father doesn't like her?"

Ida Kate shook her head. Her brown braids, neatly fixed before breakfast by Caroline's deft fingers and tied with the new ribbons Caroline had brought, swung across her shoulders like ropes. "Papa likes her very much," Ida Kate admitted, remembering the long looks and the feeling in the air that a connection had been made. "And so do I. She's such a help at home. And we took a picnic to Castle Rock on Saturday—Papa hasn't laughed so much since Mama was alive . . . and maybe not even then. Mama was a more serious type—you remember—but Caroline is always joking and smiling. She's fun to be with."

"So what *is* the trouble?" pressed Martha.

Ida Kate pulled her shawl tightly around her, feeling

a chill pour across her shoulders even though the morning was mild. "Well," she said slowly, "there are just so many things that don't add up . . . that aren't what I expected or was led to expect from her letters . . ." She bit her lip. Maybe Martha would just think she was imagining things. *But I know I'm not!*

"Do you mean to make me *beg* for the details?" asked Martha in exasperation.

"Well, for instance, Caroline sings like an angel, Martha. You should hear her! Her voice fills the house with the most wondrous songs. And as we drove home from church, she taught us some new hymns, and we sang all the way. Even the horses seemed to be trotting in time to the music."

"Sounds nice," said Martha. "Why are you worried?"

"Because Caroline Fairchild *doesn't sing*! She specifically wrote to us that she can't even carry a tune. And she's a wonderful cook, yet she wrote in her letters that she'd never learned cookery because her family had servants."

"Could be she's just very modest . . ." Martha said slowly. "Some people are blind to their own talents."

Ida Kate shook her head. "No, I don't think that's it. And there's more. She wrote that she was tall with auburn hair. But you saw her—she's short, and her hair is as brown as mine is. And, and . . . well, there's Hanky." Ida Kate felt all the confusion of the weekend swirling around inside her. In the distance the girls could now see other children on the path to the schoolhouse.

"Babies can be nuisances," Martha said. "Believe me, I am in a position to know! But Hanky seems like a sweet baby, nearly as nice as Gloria. I bet you're just not used to having a baby around."

"I don't mind having him around," Ida Kate said earnestly. "I *like* him!"

"Well, what's the trouble?" demanded Martha. "Doesn't Caroline look after him properly?"

"No, it's not that." Ida Kate frowned. She started walking faster, and Martha hurried to keep up. "Caroline is perfectly good to him, very kind and gentle. But she looks awkward holding him. And she feeds him milk from a cup rather than nursing him as mothers do, and she offers him bits of food, saying, 'Maybe he'll eat this,' as if she doesn't quite know which foods he likes." Ida Kate shook her head. "She can't get his garments on him very well and is hopeless at fastening his diapers so they stay on. *I* do a better job, and I've only ever practiced on Gloria! It's as if, oh, I don't know, sort of as if she's not used to him. I get a strange feeling when I see them together."

"Hmm," said Martha thoughtfully. Up ahead the girls could now see the schoolhouse, its thick earthen roof sprouting grass and clover. "You told me she'd had to board the baby out while she was working all the time in that factory. Maybe the baby just isn't used to his mother being with him all the time."

That made a kind of sense. Ida Kate felt relieved. She hoped Martha could just as deftly make sense of the other problems.

"Well, here's another strange thing," Ida Kate continued. "Caroline wrote to us that she came from North Carolina—but then at Castle Rock on Saturday, she said that she was from *South* Carolina!"

Martha stopped. "That *is* odd," she agreed. "How could she forget where she came from? Did you ask her about it?"

Ida Kate shook her head. "No," she murmured. "Papa heard her, too, and he didn't say anything. And then on Sunday . . ." Her voice trailed off as she remembered the strange conversation at the church luncheon. How *could* Caroline Fairchild's slave-owning father have been an abolitionist? It just didn't make sense.

The list of things that didn't make sense was much too long.

They'd reached the school yard now. Ida Kate saw the twins up ahead, and one of them—Jimmy? Johnny?—waved to her.

"I won! I won!" he yelled, pelting over to the girls. "I win the pie!"

Ida Kate duly uncovered her lunch pail and handed him the piece of apple pie Caroline had wrapped in paper. Yodeling his thanks, he sped away in a cloud of dust. The tumult of children's voices rose around them. Miss Butler came out of the schoolhouse. She stood in the doorway with her arm raised, ringing the school bell.

"Martha—there is one more thing." Ida Kate grabbed her friend's sleeve. "Caroline wrote that her husband was named Clivedon Fairchild. Then yesterday she said Hanky was named Henry *Claude*—after his father. But his middle name should be *Clivedon,* not Claude, Martha! How could somebody forget her dead husband's name? Do you think Papa would refer to Mama as *Elizabeth* instead of *Eleanor*? Of course he wouldn't!"

"My mother's name was Harriet Louise," said Martha. "There's no way my father would *ever* forget her name, even as much as he loves Margaretha now."

"So what would you think if you heard him calling your mother Hannah? Or Hortense?" cried Ida Kate.

Martha stared at Ida Kate with wide eyes. "I would say . . . I would think he had suffered a terrible blow to the head. I would think he had lost his memory. Remember when Maisie Groninger's father fell off the roof of their barn? He has no memory at all of anything from that day. He doesn't even recall that the roof had a hole in the first place."

Ida Kate's heart was thumping hard, and it wasn't just from the fast walking they'd been doing. "Papa told me about how dangerous the work in factories can be, but I don't think Caroline has suffered any recent injury. She would have told us if she had."

"Not if she couldn't remember it," Martha pointed out grimly.

A cool breeze played across the prairie grasses, and the wildflowers danced. Ida Kate, lining up with the other children and marching into the schoolhouse, felt dazed. Her doubts whirled in her head as if they, too, were being tossed by the wind.

CHAPTER 7

TEA PARTY TERROR

Miss Butler clapped her hands smartly. "Take your seats, boys and girls!" she called. She directed the children into the schoolroom. The students filed inside, all of them laughing and talking, except for Ida Kate and Martha. Ida Kate felt vaguely sick to her stomach, as if she had eaten a bad egg for breakfast. She could tell from the frown on her friend's face that Martha was troubled, too.

Ida Kate left her lunch pail with the others at the back of the room and settled into her old seat next to Martha at a long wooden table. The tables were arranged in two rows with a center aisle. Girls and boys turned to greet Ida Kate.

"We thought you'd left school forever!" called Tommy McGruder from the front of the room, where he was made to sit in the first seat under Miss Butler's watchful eye.

"Thought maybe some ol' grasshoppers had eaten

you," laughed Tommy's brother, Sam. "Crackle, crackle, crunch!"

"Crunched her up for lunch," cried Horatio Jones, clacking his teeth to demonstrate.

"Oh, ignore those awful boys," said Mae, Horatio's sister, with a toss of her long hair. "We're surely glad to have you back, Ida Kate. And that's the truth."

And Maisie and Clara Groninger, sitting at the table in front of Ida Kate, turned around and begged, "Eat lunch with us, will you, Ida Kate?"

Ida Kate smiled at everybody, even the boys. But she didn't chatter with them all as she normally did. Her head was too full of dark thoughts.

Miss Butler was standing up at the front of the classroom with her hand raised for silence. Any student who didn't obey quickly would find himself—or herself— ordered to sit in the corner wearing the "Chatterbox" sign.

"We want to welcome Ida Kate," Miss Butler began. "There have been some happy changes at home that allow her to return to us. A Mrs. Caroline Fairchild has journeyed all the way from Massachusetts to marry Mr. Deming and take over the housekeeping responsibilities that have kept Ida Kate from her studies." She nodded at Ida Kate. "I heard from my parents that they met Mrs. Fairchild at church yesterday. I do hope to meet her myself very soon."

"Thank you," Ida Kate said politely. "You must come to call."

"Yes, indeed, I should like that," said Miss Butler. "In fact, I hoped to call this very afternoon. Perhaps I might drive you home in my wagon?"

"Um—certainly, ma'am," Ida Kate said.

"Very well, then." The teacher clapped her hands. "Let us resume last week's lesson on geography. Who can name the oceans of the world?"

Ida Kate thought she knew the oceans of the world, but she was distracted by Martha's hissing: "I know my stepmother hoped to call on Caroline today. Perhaps I can come with her after school so we can work together on the mystery of Caroline Fairchild!"

The mystery of Caroline Fairchild. Those words that made Martha's voice thrum with excitement turned Ida Kate cold. Why did there have to be a mystery? Why couldn't Caroline just be the way they'd expected her to be—the way she *wrote* that she would be? Ida Kate felt a flash of anger at her father's intended bride.

Martha's hand crept over and gave Ida Kate's fingers a reassuring squeeze under the table.

After school, Ida Kate set off for home sitting high on the buckboard seat next to Miss Butler. Martha and the twins crowded in back. They stopped first at the Ruppenthals' farm to see if Martha's stepmother wanted to join their party. Mrs. Ruppenthal said yes, this would be a fine time to meet Caroline Fairchild.

Soon the Ruppenthals' cart and horse were harnessed, and the two wagons set off with Miss Butler's in the lead. Now Martha rode with her stepmother, helping to look after her three excited little siblings. The twins stayed home to get their chores done, but Mrs. Ruppenthal promised to bring them each a treat from the tea party.

At last the wagons pulled up in front of the Demings' house. Miss Butler craned her neck, looking all around as if she expected to see Caroline hiding behind a fence post. "Where is the bride?" she asked Ida Kate. "That is why we rode all the way over here—to meet this adventurous young woman. Though I must say, I find it hard to understand how anyone would travel a thousand miles to marry a man she does not know!"

Ida Kate bit back her irritation. Despite her own misgivings about Caroline, she didn't want to hear Miss Butler's criticism.

Mrs. Ruppenthal, pulling her wagon up next to Miss Butler's, cleared her throat. "Perhaps I can help you to understand," she said calmly. "I, too, traveled here to marry, though I was acquainted with Mr. Ruppenthal only through letters. You see, I came to America with my brother's family, and we settled in Pennsylvania. But I did not want to be a burden to my brother forever, and so when I learned that a good man of German descent

was advertising for a bride to come to Kansas, I felt called
to reply. I am so glad that I came to Kansas."

"We're very glad, too," said Martha loyally. "I can
barely remember my own mother. What would we do
without you? And, of course, without Gloria and Davy
and Edmund?"

Miss Butler had the grace to look ashamed. "I meant
no disrespect, Mrs. Ruppenthal. Indeed, I had forgotten
you had come to Kansas as a bride." She pursed her lips.
"You are such a pillar of the community—certainly not an
adventuress!"

Mrs. Ruppenthal nodded to show she accepted the
teacher's apology, and her lips twitched slightly. "Life
with my three little children and three big stepchildren
is definitely an adventure, I assure you," she said.

Ida Kate jumped down and ran in to alert Caroline
that company had arrived. But inside there was no sign
of Caroline, though Hanky was playing quietly under the
table with some wooden spoons. Ida Kate said hello to him,
then hurried toward the bedrooms to look for Caroline.
As she crossed the main room, Caroline emerged from
Papa's bedroom.

"Oh, you're home!" she said to Ida Kate.

"Yes," said Ida Kate, wondering if Caroline had been
dusting again. "And I've brought company. Quite a lot of
company."

"Looks like it's a good thing I spent the morning

making raisin tarts," replied Caroline, peering out the front window at all the people in the little yard, "or there would be nothing to serve."

"I hope you don't mind," Ida Kate said in a low voice. "My teacher wanted to meet you—and so did Mrs. Ruppenthal . . ."

"Of course I don't mind at all. Let's invite them in." Caroline scooped Hanky into her arms and stepped out into the yard.

Ida Kate took a deep breath to calm her jitters and managed to get the introductions out properly, the way Mama had taught her.

"Hello, my dear Mrs. Fairchild," Mrs. Ruppenthal sang out from her wagon. "I do hope this is not too late to come calling. Miss Butler and I wanted so very much to meet you. And is this your dear baby?"

"This is Hanky," said Caroline. "I'm sure he's mighty pleased to meet you." She handed Hanky to Ida Kate and reached for the horse's reins so Mrs. Ruppenthal could climb down from the cart. Martha leaped down with a single bound, Gloria in her arms.

"Martha!" reproved Mrs. Ruppenthal as she carefully stepped down. "Take care, dear." Then she patted Hanky's head. "What a sweet little boy." She handed Caroline the box containing a cake she'd baked.

Miss Butler climbed down from her wagon and presented Caroline with two jars of honey that she withdrew from her school satchel. "From my brother's own bees," Miss Butler said with pride. "My parents sell the honey at the general store."

"Thank you so much," said Caroline graciously. "Now, please come in and I shall make us some tea."

Caroline led the way into the house, followed by the Ruppenthals.

"Caroline tells me she has made raisin tarts today," Ida Kate said to her teacher as they walked together across the yard. "And I imagine they'll be very tasty. Caroline seems to be an excellent cook." Mama had always taught her that it was ladylike to know the art of conversation.

"So you address her as Caroline already, I see." Miss Butler's tone made it clear she felt this was not at all the proper thing to do.

"Yes, ma'am. She asked us to." Ida Kate stepped inside the house and set Hanky down on the floor to play.

Caroline was laying out the fine china plates that had belonged to Ida Kate's mother. She urged all the guests to find seats around the plank table. "Ida Kate, please fill this pitcher with milk from the pail."

Ida Kate took the heavy china pitcher. Martha came to the storeroom with her. She whispered in Ida Kate's ear, "Old Butler has been absolutely perishing to get a look at your mail-order bride. I wonder if she's still thinking of Caroline as an adventuress from afar coming to steal away the community's most eligible bachelor!"

Ida Kate rolled her eyes at Martha. She used the dipper to fill the pitcher with milk and then took the milk to the table. Caroline was serving the raisin tarts and slices of Mrs. Ruppenthal's cake. Mrs. Ruppenthal sat with Gloria nestled on her lap and fed the toddler small pieces. Davy and Edmund sat next to their mother on the trestle bench, swinging their legs.

When everyone was served, Caroline settled Hanky on her lap and began to eat. Ida Kate, watching her, saw that she didn't cuddle him close the way Mrs. Ruppenthal held Gloria. She held him stiffly, as if unsure what to do with him. It was just as Ida Kate had described to Martha earlier. Ida Kate clenched her hands together on her lap, wishing she could discover what it all meant.

"Mama?" asked Hanky. He screwed up his face and started to cry.

"Oh, dear," said Caroline. "He gets very cranky without his nap. Ida Kate, would you try to settle him down?"

Ida Kate took the fussy baby and excused herself. In the bedroom she changed his diaper—loose again!—and rocked him in her arms, patting him firmly on the back until he closed his eyes. Then she lowered him gently into the little crib.

When Ida Kate returned, she found Caroline pouring more tea, all the while speaking eagerly, asking the other two women about life on the prairie, about Hays City, about their families.

Mrs. Ruppenthal was speaking to Caroline as if they were old friends. Even Miss Butler seemed less sour about the newcomer now that they were having tea together.

As the women talked, Ida Kate watched Caroline carefully, searching for some sign of grievous injury that might cause memory lapses. She saw nothing unusual.

"But enough about us," Mrs. Ruppenthal said as Caroline offered everyone another raisin tart. "Let us hear about you. Tell us all about yourself!"

"Oh, there's not much that's especially interesting," Caroline demurred with a smile. "I'm a southern girl by birth, then moved to Massachusetts after my husband died. Factory work is grueling, ladies, and I wouldn't recommend it to anyone."

"Where in the South?" Miss Butler asked sharply. "Your family weren't slave owners, were they? We don't hold with slavery out here in Kansas, you know. Kansas entered the Union as a free state from the very beginning!"

"Now, Miss Butler," said Mrs. Ruppenthal. "The War Between the States has been over for more than ten years. There's no use bringing it up."

"My father owned a plantation in—ah—North Caro-lina," Caroline said softly, "and he did own slaves. But I'm glad to say he emancipated them and then paid them to continue working for us. Still, by the end of the war, we'd lost our home and land, and—worst of all—my father and two brothers had been killed."

"I am sorry to hear that," said Miss Butler, pressing her napkin neatly to her mouth to catch a cake crumb. "I also lost a brother in the war. He was fighting for the North, however, I'm proud to say."

"And your husband was a soldier, too?" Mrs. Ruppenthal interjected quickly, turning to Caroline.

"He was wounded in the chest," said Caroline. She had a faraway look in her eyes, as if she was trying to remember. Ida Kate narrowed her eyes as she listened.

"A grievous lung injury," Caroline continued, shaking her head sadly. "But we weren't married at the time; we didn't marry until after the war. He was a distant cousin of mine. Our mothers hoped that we would marry, so finally we did. But he never really recovered his strength after his injury. First his own mother died, and my mother and I tried to earn our living as seamstresses, but we weren't very good ones, I'm afraid. My husband worked whenever he could at the land surveyor's office, but with his bad lungs, he was too ill to work as often as not. Then my mother died of influenza, and consumption set into my poor husband's lungs and he died as well. He never even knew I was expecting our baby." She sat quietly, looking down at her hands.

"Oh, what a very tragic story," said Mrs. Ruppenthal sympathetically, and even Ida Kate felt moved by Caroline's account. "Let us hope your life has taken a turn for the better now."

"Oh, I'm sure it has!" Caroline's solemn face broke into a smile. "I waited until the baby was born, then moved to Lynn, Massachusetts. I had to leave Hanky with a baby minder all day while I worked in the factory. Mr. Deming's advertisement seemed like a beacon, pointing the way west to a better life. I am so very glad we've come!"

"We're glad, also," said Mrs. Ruppenthal.

Then Caroline ate the last bite of her cake and laid down her fork. "I do declare, that was such delicious cake, Mrs. Ruppenthal," she said, and Ida Kate noticed the southern accent was more pronounced than before. "You simply must give me the recipe—unless it is a closely guarded family secret."

"I will be happy to share it with you right now. Indeed, the cake is ever so simple to make, and I've got the recipe memorized. And please do call me Margaretha, since we are now neighbors—and our girls such dear friends."

Caroline smiled across the table at Ida Kate. "Ida Kate, would you mind finding me a scrap of paper, a pen, and some ink? I shall ask Mrs. Ruppenthal—Margaretha!—to copy the recipe while her cake is still melting in my mouth."

Ida Kate obediently left the table and went into Papa's bedroom. She walked straight to his dresser and opened the small wooden box where he kept their paper, pens, and ink bottle. And, of course, the letters from Caroline.

She lifted out the packet and saw immediately that the ribbon was not in its proper bow but was simply knotted. Ida Kate's forehead creased in a frown as she slipped off the ribbon. Caroline *had* been snooping.

Ida Kate fanned through the letters, thinking how amazing it was that once Caroline Fairchild had been only words on the page—and now she was here, real and bright and large as life, right out at the table. Ida Kate did not feel *she* was snooping when she opened the first letter, because she and Papa had shared each letter as it arrived.

Dear Sir, began the first letter they'd received from Caroline in her elegant, angled writing that marched so neatly across the page. The second letter started off *Dear Mr. Deming.* The salutation on the third read *Dear Henry,* and finally on later ones (Ida Kate shuffled rapidly through the remaining few letters), *My dear husband-to-be.* It was a sweet story, Ida Kate thought, folding the letters again and replacing the ribbon—or at least it had started out to be.

If only she didn't have such worries about Caroline. If only Caroline would stop snooping and making such strange mistakes! Was her behavior really due to lost memory—or was something sinister going on?

Ida Kate grabbed the pen, the ink bottle, and a sheet of paper and shut the wooden box with a hard snap, as if she could shut off her disturbing thoughts in a similar

fashion. Then she hurried back to the tea party and set the
writing things on the table in front of Mrs. Ruppenthal.
Miss Butler was talking quietly to Martha about the poem
Martha would be reciting at the school picnic next month.
Edmund and Davy were stacking the smooth wooden
blocks that Papa had made for Ida Kate when she was
little. Then Gloria toddled over and knocked the castle
down. The boys shouted at her and she began howling.
Then she started throwing the blocks.

"Oh, dear," said Mrs. Ruppenthal, hurrying over to
pick up the little girl. "I think we have overstayed our
welcome, my sweet one."

Caroline uncapped the bottle of ink and held out the
pen. "Please don't leave without writing down the recipe,"
she said. "I have never tasted such a cake."

"Certainly," said Mrs. Ruppenthal, balancing the
screeching Gloria on one ample hip. "But now that my
hands are full, I shall dictate it to you. You begin with
one pound of flour . . ."

Caroline looked flustered. She turned to Ida Kate.
"Would you care to write it for me, dear? I think I heard
Hanky waking up." She dipped the pen into the ink and
held it out.

Ida Kate shook her head, puzzled. "I don't hear him.
I'm sure he's still fast asleep."

Caroline bit her lip. She hunched over the paper
and began to write as Mrs. Ruppenthal's voice enunciated

each ingredient clearly: a pound of flour, a pound of butter, a pound of sugar, six eggs . . . all mixed well and set
into a hot oven with . . .

Ida Kate's heart began to pound as she watched
Caroline's pen move across the paper. What she saw
made her hands grow cold even though the day was
still warm.

Caroline finished writing and blotted the ink carefully. "I shall try my hand at this cake very soon," she said
brightly. "You'll like that, won't you, Ida Kate?" She
glanced up to find Ida Kate staring at her. A deep flush
slowly spread up Caroline's neck to her cheeks as their
eyes met. Hastily she folded the recipe and tucked it into
her apron hanging on the hook by the stove.

Caroline walked her guests out to the wagons, but
Ida Kate just called good-bye from the door. She could
hear Caroline thanking everyone for coming and urging
them to return soon. Their voices rang cheerfully outside
in the yard, but to Ida Kate, standing inside by the stove,
they sounded hollow.

She reached quickly for the apron hanging on its hook.
She fished the folded recipe out of the pocket.

"Hey," Martha called to her from the doorway. "Aren't
you even going to see us off?" Then, noting Ida Kate's
expression, she hurried to her friend's side. "What's wrong?"

Wordlessly Ida Kate unfolded the recipe. Her heart
thumped hard as she held it out.

Dear Sir, Caroline had written in her lengthy letters to Papa. *Dear Mr. Deming. Dear Henry. My dear husband-to-be.* But where was the elegantly slanted handwriting now?

Pound of Flower, Buter, Shuger, Eggs, Milk . . . The cake recipe was written in a heavy black scrawl, the letters ill-formed, the spelling as often wrong as it was right.

Ida Kate crammed the recipe into her own pocket and stared at Martha.

"What's wrong?" whispered Martha. "I mean, besides the spelling?"

Ida Kate shook her head. "You'd better go. They're calling for you." She was desperate now for Martha to leave, for everyone to leave. She was desperate to be out of sight when Caroline came back into the house. "Hurry and go. I'll talk to you at school tomorrow. I promise!"

And as Martha, perplexed, left the house, Ida Kate slipped into the darkness of the storeroom. She carefully shut the door and leaned against it, her thoughts spinning. She listened intently for Papa's heavy step coming into the house. But she heard other things instead. She heard someone else.

She heard pots banging around as someone prepared the evening meal. She heard teacups clattering as someone cleared the table.

Someone was out there. Someone who had come on a train from far away—bringing a baby boy and settling right in. Someone who had very nicely arranged her silver-backed hairbrush and comb on Ida Kate's bureau and hung her garments on the pegs along Ida Kate's walls. Someone who was using Mama's cooking pots and pretty china and liked to go walking out in the fields with Papa, leaning on his arm. *Someone.*

Someone—but not Caroline Fairchild. Ida Kate could no longer deny the terrible truth, and it was all she could do to keep from screaming.

The woman they all called Caroline Fairchild was an *impostor.*

CHAPTER 8
IMPOSTOR!

"An impostor?" cried Martha the next morning on the way to school. "Oh, mercy, are you *sure?*"

"Shhh!" Ida Kate shook Martha's arm. The twins were ambling along just ahead, and she didn't want anyone else overhearing this conversation. She couldn't even really believe they were having this conversation in the first place.

"Are you very sure?" pressed Martha in a softer voice.

"Look at *this,*" said Ida Kate, pulling the cake recipe out of one pocket of her pinafore. "And compare it with *this.*" She reached into the other pocket and withdrew a folded letter. She shook it open and handed both letter and recipe to Martha. "Compare the handwriting. That's all you need to do to see that the same person couldn't have written both."

Martha scanned the recipe and the letter and sucked in her breath sharply. "I see what you mean," she murmured.

"But maybe she was ashamed that her handwriting and spelling are so poor, so she asked a friend from her factory—somebody with elegant handwriting—to help, and she *dictated* the letters she sent your father. That's not a crime . . ."

"But why would the daughter of a wealthy southern planter have such terrible penmanship in the first place?" demanded Ida Kate. "No, Martha, I just don't believe it. Not when you consider all the other strange things about her."

Martha's eyes gleamed with excitement. "Then you must be right, Ida Kate! She *is* an impostor!"

Ida Kate twisted her braid in agitation. She wanted to find a simple, agreeable explanation for the strange handwriting and be done with it. She'd lain awake for hours last night trying to come up with some innocent explanation that would account for all the strange mistakes Caroline kept making. But there wasn't one.

Ida Kate heaved a deep sigh. Too many mistakes altogether.

"Ooh, it makes me shiver," breathed Martha. "What will you do?"

"I have to tell Papa, of course," Ida Kate said firmly. "I wanted to tell him last night, but I was never alone with him."

"Why didn't you just announce it at the dinner table?" asked Martha.

"I don't know," Ida Kate said softly. She scuffed her boots along the track and watched the dust fly up. "I just couldn't, somehow, not in front of *her.*"

"Well, I think you're probably right to stay quiet for a while," Martha replied slowly. "Because someone who can pull a ruse like this is very clever—and probably dangerous, too. And your father is so sweet on her, he'll likely think you're just turning against her because you don't want another woman taking your mother's place. It will be the impostor's word against yours, and he's not going to want to believe you. So you need to uncover more facts. And *then* you can confront her—and your father will have to believe."

"I still think these handwriting samples are pretty strong proof . . ." began Ida Kate. But Martha was shaking her head.

"We'll need to find even better proof. I know! We'll go to your house after school and try to discover more facts about this—this *stranger.* Then, once we know what's what, we can tell your father in time to stop him from marrying a fraud! What do you say, Ida Kate?"

Ida Kate usually loved following Martha into adventure, riding along on her friend's enthusiasm. But now Ida Kate simply felt exhausted. And underneath her fatigue was sadness. She had liked Caroline Fairchild— liked her very much indeed. That Caroline was not who she said she was seemed a terrible betrayal.

"I still think I should just tell Papa," Ida Kate mumbled.

"Not yet! Not till we investigate," Martha pressed. "After all, if the woman living in your house isn't Caroline, then shouldn't we find out where the *real* Caroline Fairchild is? Your father will certainly want to know. We should wait to tell him until we have proof of who this woman and the baby really are."

"What do you mean?" asked Ida Kate, a quiet dread welling up inside her. "The baby is just Hanky—" But then she broke off. *Oh no.*

What if the baby isn't really Hanky at all?

If the woman wasn't the real Caroline Fairchild, then how could the baby be Caroline's baby? Or—had the impostor somehow kidnapped Hanky from the real Caroline? That would explain the strange awkwardness Ida Kate had noticed between the false Caroline and the baby.

A shiver slithered down Ida Kate's back. Was the real Caroline searching even now for her baby? For surely a mother would come searching—unless she *couldn't* . . .

They had reached the school yard now and heard the shouts of their friends greeting them. Martha raised her arm in a cheerful wave, but Ida Kate could barely smile.

The thought thudded in her head: *What has become of the real Caroline?*

The morning passed in a march of the usual subjects—
geography, arithmetic, recitation, and spelling—but Ida
Kate couldn't concentrate. Miss Butler frowned at her
when she misspelled the word *outrageous* during the spelling bee. At lunchtime Ida Kate and Martha carried their
lunch pails to their favorite bench behind the school
building. Mabel, Maisie, and Clara all came running to sit
with them, full of questions about Ida Kate's mail-order
bride. But Ida Kate didn't want to talk about Caroline
with the other girls. She gave Martha a kick on the ankle
to warn her to keep her mouth shut.

Martha kicked her back, and Ida Kate winced.

"When is the wedding?" asked Mabel. "May we all
come?"

"Ooh! I love weddings!" squealed Clara. "Will you be
her bridesmaid?"

But there would be no wedding, Ida Kate realized
sadly. Papa must not marry somebody who was only
posing as Caroline Fairchild.

The afternoon of lessons dragged on, until finally
Ida Kate and Martha were on their way home. Martha's
twin brothers raced ahead, but the girls walked slowly.
Ida Kate watched the prairie grasses blowing in the wind.

"What I can't understand," Martha began, "is why
someone would bother pretending to be someone else."

"I'm figuring she must want something," Ida Kate
replied. "Something she thinks Papa can give her."

"Marriage? A farm on the prairie? What?" asked Martha.

"I think she wants his fortune."

"Does he *have* a fortune?" gasped Martha.

"No—but maybe the impostor thinks he does. When Caroline Fairchild wrote that she'd been a wealthy southern girl until the War Between the States, Papa replied that he, too, had been brought up in luxury—until he gave it all up to follow his dream of working the land. Papa probably isn't ever going to see a penny of Grandfather's money—and he doesn't care."

"So why do you think this impostor wants to marry him for a fortune he won't ever have?" asked Martha, her voice puzzled.

"Maybe she believes my grandfather will change his mind. After all, he's still alive back in Philadelphia. She might know that."

"Hmmm," said Martha. "But didn't you say she'd been living in some factory town in Massachusetts? Not Philadelphia."

"The real Caroline Fairchild was living in Massachusetts. Who knows where this stranger has been living!" Ida Kate stared around her at the billowing grasses. She knew that all sorts of animals made their homes beneath the prairie grasses, hidden from sight. Where was the real Caroline Fairchild hidden away right now?

Ida Kate watched a jackrabbit leap through the rustling grasses and bound away into the distance. Was this impostor also running from something?

It was as if Martha had read her mind. "I know! Perhaps she's a criminal escaping from justice! She did away with the real Caroline, took the baby, and now she's on the run. When she marries and takes the name of Deming, the law won't be able to track her down . . ."

"Maybe," said Ida Kate slowly. She rubbed her hand over her forehead and felt the furrows of a deep frown. It all sounded so improbable that Caroline Fairchild should be anything but what she said she was: a young woman coming to Kansas to marry the man she'd promised to marry. And yet . . . What to do about it? How to trap an impostor? How to keep Papa from marrying the wrong woman?

They had reached the turnoff for the Hays City track. A wagon loaded with hay was lumbering toward them, and they had to skip to the side of the road to let it pass. The driver was Jack Groninger, Maisie's oldest brother, who tipped his hat to them and called down, "Good afternoon, ladies!"

"Good afternoon," Ida Kate said politely, but Martha sang out the little rhyme that children always called when they saw a hay wagon:

"Load of hay, load of hay!
Make a wish and turn away!"

Laughing, Martha turned her back on Jack until the

wagon had passed.

"What did you wish?" asked Ida Kate. She had forgotten to make a wish. And anyway, what would she wish
for? That the impostor would turn out to be Caroline
after all? That Ida Kate would wake up and find this was
all a dream and the mail-order bride hadn't even arrived
at the depot yet? That—somehow—Mama hadn't died
during that blizzard, and so there had never been any
thought of a new bride?

"I wished we would solve the riddle of Caroline
Fairchild this very day," said Martha. "And what did you
wish?"

"I didn't wish anything," Ida Kate admitted. She
resumed walking along with Martha at her side. "But I
wish I had. I would wish most of all that Papa won't get
hurt. It's so wonderful seeing him happy again."

"Well, let's make my wish come true, and then maybe
yours can come true."

"What do you mean?" asked Ida Kate.

"I mean let me come home with you now," Martha
begged. "We can start by searching her belongings . . ."

Snooping . . . the way the impostor was already snooping around their house. *It's fighting fire with fire!* Ida Kate
decided. Snooping wasn't snooping if it was for a good
cause. Her anger, slow to start, was fanning out now like a
prairie brushfire. How dare someone come into Ida Kate
and Papa's home and pretend to be someone else!

Martha's eyes were sparkling the way they always did when she was playing a game and hoped to win. But fingers of fear fluttered up Ida Kate's spine despite her surge of righteous anger, for she knew this was no game.

This was really happening, and it was happening to Ida Kate and Papa. The woman in their house was a liar and a stranger—somebody they did not really know at all. Somebody who would not want to be unmasked.

CHAPTER 9
THE BATTLE FOR TRUTH

 Just over the next rise, the girls reached Martha's sod house, and Martha ran inside for permission to walk on with Ida Kate. She would not stay long, she promised her stepmother. Please, please? She would come home by suppertime and would make up for not doing her chores by playing with baby Gloria until bedtime.

Ida Kate listened to her friend cajole Mrs. Ruppenthal and wished she, too, might someday have the same sort of easygoing relationship with a stepmother. If only Caroline were the one . . . But such thoughts were useless now.

The girls left Martha's house holding pieces of corn-bread. "For strength," Martha said solemnly, biting into her snack. "As we go into battle!"

"It's not a *battle,* Martha," interrupted Ida Kate. People were killed in battles.

"Oh, yes—it's a battle for Truth!"

Ida Kate wished Martha were not so eager to take action. But as the girls trudged on, Ida Kate's spirits rose. Papa had gone to war for something he believed in. Ida Kate would fight *this* battle, for she believed that Papa must not be duped.

The grasses on either side of the track swished back and forth in the wind. Ida Kate could hear humming in the grass and hoped the grasshoppers weren't back. But maybe a plague of grasshoppers would be the very thing they needed—something to scare the bride away before they had to confront her.

The girls reached the Deming homestead and saw Papa leading the two milk cows back from the far field, where they had been grazing with the other cattle. Old Hickory was at Papa's side but broke into a run when he saw Ida Kate. Papa waved to the girls as he reached the barnyard. "Hello there," he called. "How was school?"

"It was just fine, Papa," Ida Kate called back.

"I'm sure you're enjoying seeing your friends again," Papa said. The cows stamped their feet and blew out of their big, soft noses. "I was just back at the house telling Caroline that you had probably stopped at Martha's house on your way home—but I see you've brought Martha to us instead. Run along now to Caroline; I'm sure there's something good to eat. That accomplished lady has been baking again today, and there's something

bubbling in the stew pot that surely does smell delicious."
He rubbed his hands together. "Caroline will spoil us
entirely, Ida Kate, I have no doubt about it." He beamed
at the girls, happiness shining in his eyes.

Ida Kate gave Papa a quick hug. He smelled of sweat
and animals, and his dark beard tickled her cheek. She
thought how much she loved him, how good he was, and
how she would *not* let some false bride hurt him.

Help me, Mama! Show me what to do!

"Come out to the barn when you're through in the
house," Papa said, "and I'll harness up Thunder and drive
Martha back home while you help get supper ready."

"Yes, Papa," said Ida Kate. *You keep watch over Papa, too,
don't you, Mama? You won't let anyone hurt him, will you?*

"Thank you, Mr. Deming," said Martha. "Thunder
is so strong and fast, he probably really *can* run me home
and return to his stall before Ida Kate gets done with
her chores!"

"We'll test him on that," promised Papa, his black
beard twitching as he smiled.

The girls walked on toward the house with Old Hickory
bounding along. "Stay outside," Ida Kate whispered to
the dog. "Good boy."

She took a deep breath and opened the door. There
was no one standing over the stove, although the delicious
smell Papa had spoken of wafted toward them from the
bubbling cast-iron pot. There was no baby playing on the

blanket spread near the window. The girls entered the house and shut the door quietly. They stood there listening. All was silent.

Ida Kate had a sudden, terrible certainty that danger lurked in this silence. She tried to summon back the feeling that her mama was hovering close by—an angel with wings outstretched—but the feeling was gone.

There was a faint mewing sound from Caroline's bedroom. Caroline must be with the baby, Ida Kate decided, and she bravely led the way to say hello. The important thing now was to act as if everything were normal, as if there were no suspicions. Then, when the impostor was busy somewhere else, they would search through her things.

The door to Caroline's bedroom was ajar, so Ida Kate pushed the door open silently. Millie the kitten slept curled on the bed's blue and white coverlet—the one carefully quilted by Ida Kate's mother. The mirror over the dresser reflected the otherwise empty room.

But no—not empty after all: little Hanky snored gently in the crib. He stirred as they watched him. Ida Kate stared down at him, searching for a resemblance to the woman who called herself his mother. The baby had red curls; his mother's hair was straight and brown. But maybe the father's hair had been red . . . ?

"Caroline's not here," whispered Ida Kate. "She's probably in Papa's room again, reading the letters the real Caroline wrote so that she'll know the details of

the part she's playing!" Ida Kate's heart thudded. Would
Caroline notice that one of the letters was missing? The
one Ida Kate had taken to show Martha was folded up in
Ida Kate's pinafore pocket along with the recipe.

"Perhaps she's just gone out to the privy," Martha said.
She moved to peer out the window. "No, there she is—
over in the vegetable garden! We won't have much time. Is
this where she sleeps?"

"Yes," whispered Ida Kate. "Now we must hurry. You
guard the door, and I'll get started." Ida Kate slid open
the top dresser drawer. "While she's out—it's our perfect
chance."

"Oh, Ida Kate . . ." Martha, usually so brave, looked
nervous. But she walked over and carefully closed the
bedroom door till only a crack remained through which
she could peer out.

Ida Kate could feel her heartbeat now, rhythmically
thumping in her chest. She knew she would have to search
fast. *It would be a great help to know* what *I was searching for,*
she thought, then took a deep breath and set to work.

She lifted out the folded garments and checked inside
the layers of clothing and in the corners of the drawers.
She found nothing unusual. She quickly explored the
pockets of Caroline's three dresses and woolen coat hanging on the pegs along the wall. Nothing there, either.

Ida Kate hurriedly sifted through the things laid
out on the dresser top: the hairbrush and comb, two

tortoiseshell hair combs, a bottle of rose water, a pair of sharp sewing scissors, a small, heart-shaped china dish with a lid—only pins and a slender brass key inside—and a toothbrush standing in a glass next to a tin of tooth powder. Nothing more.

Out the window now there was no sign of Caroline. What if Caroline were coming in? What excuse could Ida Kate make for being in here? Perhaps she could say she was looking for a book she'd left behind when she'd moved to the storeroom? Anxiety made Ida Kate feel shaky, but she pressed on with her search.

She crossed to the large trunk standing beneath the window. She tried to lift the heavy lid, but it was locked. *Of course,* she thought. People who had something to hide wouldn't just leave it out to be found! "Martha," she whispered. "The trunk is locked."

"There must be a key . . ." Martha hissed from her post by the door.

"And there is!" whispered Ida Kate. She ran to scoop the brass key out of the heart-shaped dish on the dresser.

Then Hanky stirred again, and she sucked in her breath raggedly. What if Caroline heard him! Ida Kate felt faint, sure they would be caught at any second.

Martha spoke up from her post at the door, shaking her head as Ida Kate fitted the key into the trunk. "Well, there won't be anything important hidden in there if she's just left the key right on the dresser . . ."

And when Ida Kate opened the heavy lid of the trunk, all she found were some folded blankets smelling of cedar, some crocheted tablecloths, and a pair of woolen gloves. She searched quickly through the folds of the blankets, but again found nothing.

Martha snorted in disgust. "Neat as a pin and completely innocent. But how come I don't believe it?"

"I don't believe it either," said Ida Kate, replacing everything into the trunk. "Let's keep looking." There had to be *something* here that would prove who their visitor really was.

Anger surged in Ida Kate again. She shouldn't have to feel so frightened in her own house. She shouldn't have to creep around like a criminal, furtive and anxious. She scanned the room. What had they overlooked?

With a flash of inspiration, she knelt beside the bed and pulled up the coverlet to peer underneath. *Aha!*

The reticule.

Ida Kate pulled it out, hissing for Martha to help. Martha closed the door firmly, and then they knelt together next to the bed and unbuckled the stiff leather straps of the heavy canvas bag. Then they lifted out the contents piece by piece: A thick photograph album covered in elegant blue velvet. A large round tin, its top printed with a picture of swans on a lake and the words *Kauffman's Finest Biscuits.* And last of all, a small object wrapped in green felt.

Ida Kate unwrapped the felt bundle—and gasped. She was holding a dagger.

It was a small, very sharp looking dagger with a gleaming silver blade and a carved wooden handle. The carving was a vine, with lacy little leaves—a strangely pleasant sort of decoration on something so lethal, she thought.

Then she heard footsteps outside the bedroom door. She and Martha frantically shoved the reticule, album, and tin box under the bed just as the latch was lifting. Ida Kate dropped the dagger into her pinafore pocket as the door opened and Caroline stepped inside.

"Oh!" Caroline cried in surprise.

"We thought we heard Hanky," Martha said loudly. "He started to fuss."

All three of them glanced at the crib, where Hanky, his nap disturbed now, was stretching and moving under his cotton blanket. "I didn't hear you come in from school," Caroline said slowly. Was Ida Kate imagining it, or did the woman sound suspicious?

"I called hello when we came in," Ida Kate invented quickly. "I called, but you didn't answer, so we thought you must be in here with the baby, and then when we got to the door, we heard him cry, as Martha said, and so we came in to get him."

Martha whirled over to the crib and smiled gaily down at the baby. "Hello, little lamb," she crooned, then flashed a bright smile back at Caroline. "He's *sooo* precious! May I please hold him?"

Caroline nodded, distracted. Her gaze swept over Ida Kate. Could Caroline tell that Ida Kate had the dagger in her pocket? Ida Kate's blood felt like ice in her veins. She gave what she meant to be a cheerful little laugh, but it came out sounding rather like the cluck of one of their hens. "Shall I change his diaper?" she asked. "How long has he been napping?"

"About an hour," Caroline said. "Enough for me to get some weeding done in the garden. And—yes, please do get him ready. I'll cut some slices of bread if you're hungry. And there's freshly churned butter . . ."

"Thank you!" Martha lifted Hanky into her arms and nuzzled his cheek.

"That sounds good," Ida Kate said weakly. "I'm surely famished."

Caroline gave her a long look, then left the room. In a flash, Ida Kate raced over and shut the door. Martha placed Hanky back in the crib and knelt on the floor by the bed. She dragged out the reticule.

"Oh, Martha, not now!" protested Ida Kate in a whisper.

"Of course now," Martha whispered back. "While she's busy."

Martha opened the cover of the photograph album, and Ida Kate pressed close to see. The sepia-tone photographs had been slipped into openings in the heavy cardboard

pages so that each photograph appeared to be framed, like
a painting, in an ornately decorated mounting. There was
only one photograph per page. Most were portraits of
bearded men in uniforms or pictures of stern-faced ladies
dressed in black standing next to formal bouquets of flowers. There were a few photographs of children in ruffles
and lace, sitting astride a wooden rocking horse or holding a toy sailboat or doll, all gazing without expression
into the distance. There was one photograph of a chubby
baby sitting in a wicker pram. The baby looked older
than Hanky and didn't have his curly hair. There were
no names penned in the album identifying any of these
people. Ida Kate closed the photograph album.

Hanky pulled himself up in the crib, banging his hands
on the top rail. "Could you change his diaper, Martha?"
Ida Kate murmured. "Otherwise he'll start to howl and
Caroline will come back!" She was replacing the album
in the reticule when a loose photograph slipped out from
the back. She picked it up and stared.

The picture was faded and a bit blurry. It was of two
young women, standing with their arms about each other
in a casual, friendly pose. One of the women was the
impostor! Both wore big white aprons over their dresses.
The hair of the woman Ida Kate knew as Caroline was
messy, as if wind were blowing. She wore no hat. Neither
did the other woman, who was taller than Caroline, and
thin. Her hair, a long, thick braid, was wrapped around the

top of her head and pinned into place. The background was a fanciful landscape of tall mountains and lush valleys, clearly painted, not real.

Caroline and this other woman appeared to be friends, Ida Kate decided, even though the smiles on their faces looked frozen—as smiles in photographs always did, since it took so long for the studio photographer to take the picture. Ida Kate turned the photograph over. On the back, written in the elegant handwriting Ida Kate recognized from Caroline's letters, were the words *Lucy and Caroline—two working girls!*

Ida Kate frowned, trying to puzzle it out. The shorter woman was recognizable as the very same Caroline who was preparing their snack in the other room. The taller one wearing the coiled braid like a crown was unfamiliar. The handwriting on the back belonged to whoever had written the letters to Ida Kate and her father. Yet the Caroline Ida Kate knew did not write such a fine hand.

Lucy and Caroline. But which was which?

Ida Kate held out the photograph for Martha, who was standing by with a freshly diapered Hanky in her arms. "Hmm," said Martha thoughtfully, studying it.

Ida Kate slipped the picture into the deep pocket of her pinafore along with the dagger, the letter, and the recipe. She was gathering quite a collection of stolen goods. *Evidence,* she told herself resolutely. *For showing to Papa.*

She quickly put the album back in the reticule and

was shoving it under the bed when Martha's voice stopped her. "Wait—there's still the tin!"

Ida Kate picked up the round tin. Quickly she levered off the lid. She and Martha stared down in astonishment at what was inside: not Kauffman's Finest Biscuits at all, but a thick, coiled braid of auburn hair, tied at each end with a blue hair ribbon.

A strange hush settled over the bedroom as Ida Kate slowly withdrew the photograph from her pinafore pocket. Yes—there was the same sort of braid wrapped around the unknown woman's head.

The girls looked at each other. Could it really be the same braid—and what if it were? What did this mean? Why would Caroline have brought her friend's long hair to Kansas?

Her tall, thin friend's long, auburn hair.

So—was the woman wearing the braid in the picture the real Caroline Fairchild? But that would mean the other woman, the one they recognized, was somebody named Lucy.

Why would Lucy come to Kansas pretending to be Caroline? Why would she hide her friend's hair away under the bed? Why would the real Caroline have given Lucy the long, beautiful braid, anyway? And if it hadn't been given . . . could it have been *taken*?

Hesitantly, as if reaching for something that could prove quite dangerous, Ida Kate lifted the heavy braid out of the tin and held it up at arm's length. It was very long, almost three feet. And beneath it in the bottom of the tin was a packet of letters tied with string.

With a stifled cry, Ida Kate dropped the braid and snatched up the letters. She recognized these letters. These were the very letters she and Papa had sent to Caroline Fairchild.

Ida Kate turned to Martha with wide, troubled eyes. "I can scarcely believe . . ." she began in a whisper.

"Yes, you can," Martha whispered back, her eyes glinting with fearful excitement. "And I believe it, too!" She reached out and stroked the braid with one trembling finger. "I believe your mail-order bride isn't merely an impostor . . . she is a *murderess.*"

Ida Kate pressed her hand hard against her mouth. But why else had the woman with the braid not come searching for her stolen baby? Surely she would be searching everywhere—if she were still alive.

Little Hanky leaned forward in Martha's arms, trying to grab the length of hair. When Martha held it out of reach, he lunged for the photograph in Ida Kate's hand. "Mama?" he said. "Mama!"

CHAPTER 10
MURDERESS!

The little house seemed to pulse with tension as Ida Kate and Martha sat eating their fresh bread and butter at the table, with Hanky on Ida Kate's lap and the impostor— Lucy!—stirring the pot of stew on the stove.

Ida Kate felt she couldn't bear for Martha to leave. "Can't you sleep here?" she muttered.

But Martha shook her head vehemently, her mouth full of bread. "No, your father is going to take me back soon." She glanced furtively over at the impostor at the stove. "I think it might be . . . better . . . if *you* slept at my house instead."

She means it would be safer, thought Ida Kate. She looked desperately around the little house, wishing for Papa. And just then she heard the latch on the door. In came Papa. He smiled at everyone. "What a lovely sight! Three fine ladies and one little imp." He lifted

Hanky off Ida Kate's lap and tossed him high in the air.
"And the incomparable smell of freshly baked bread. Not
to mention the scent of your stew, Caroline, my dear.
Bottle it as perfume and make your fortune!"

Ida Kate's stomach clenched at her father's happiness.

Caroline—the false Caroline—laughed gaily at Papa's
remarks. "I doubt many ladies would care to go about
smelling of chicken stew!" she said, then added sweetly,
"The promise of such a husband as you is fortune enough
for me."

They gazed at each other for a long moment while
Martha kicked Ida Kate sharply under the table and
whispered, "See? See? She *does* think she'll be rich once
she marries him . . ."

"I don't think that's what she meant," Ida Kate
began—when Papa interrupted.

"Well, Princess Martha, your carriage awaits. I've
hitched up Thunder, and I'll need to take you home right
now so that I get back in time for my chicken stew."

"I'll come, too, Papa!" said Ida Kate, hurriedly standing up. She did not want to be left with the impostor—
not even for the half hour it would take Papa to drive
Martha home and return.

"I'd like you to stay with me," said the impostor.
"You can mind Hanky while I fry up the apple fritters."

"Mmm, yes indeed," Papa said. "Stay with Caroline.
I need those fritters!"

"But, Papa!" Ida Kate blinked back sudden tears.

Martha squeezed Ida Kate's hand. "See you at school tomorrow," she said, but her expression was mournful. "Good luck." She flushed. "I mean, good-bye!"

When Papa and Martha had driven off, a strained silence settled over the little house. Ida Kate played with Hanky, building him little towers of wooden blocks to knock over. She peeled apples and started to slice them—but the impostor stopped her.

"Here," she said, handing her another knife. "Use this one. A sharp knife is very important."

Very important for cutting off people's hair after you've stabbed them to death with your dagger?

Ida Kate watched the false Caroline wield another sharp knife, snapping through the innocent apples. She saw again in her mind the way this impostor had sliced through the rattlesnake. *Was that how easily you might slice your victim's neck?*

It seemed to her now that the false Caroline's expression was furtive. Every motion and every word took on new and dreadful significance. Ida Kate was hugely relieved when Papa returned.

They sat down to supper together, and the stew was delicious. Papa and his intended bride leaned their heads close together as they talked about their day, sharing jokes, laughing together. Ida Kate could tell that her beloved Papa had fallen in love with this woman. She knew he

had hoped for a pleasant partnership with his new bride—
the sort of partnership that made up so many frontier
marriages—but he had not expected to find love again
after Mama's death. Their wedding date was set already,
just two weeks away.

If Ida Kate did not warn Papa, his very life might be
in danger. A person who had killed once would not hesi-
tate to kill again.

The fact that the impostor was still at large must mean
that the death of the real Caroline had appeared accidental. A brutal stabbing would not have been easy to hide . . .
Ida Kate's thoughts were racing now. The impostor might
be very good indeed at arranging "accidents." She might
be a strangler, or a poisoner . . . Ida Kate looked at the
impostor's strong hands spooning up stew for Hanky. She
looked down at her own bowl. She couldn't eat another
bite of stew.

It was too much to bear when, later that evening,
Papa asked for a haircut, and the false Caroline brought
out the sharp scissors from the bedroom.

Ida Kate stood watching, hands clenched into fists,
as her father sat at the table with a towel wrapped around
his neck to catch the hair. The false Caroline stood over
him, sharp scissors poised, and surveyed her intended
husband. She reached out—Ida Kate flinched—and
snipped at his beard.

"This needs just a little trim," she said. "That's all."

Then she set about cutting his shaggy dark mane of hair. "Watch out," Papa joked as she snipped around his sideburns. "You nearly took my ear right off!"

He caught her fingers, and Ida Kate watched as he held them tenderly for a moment. Then the woman he thought was Caroline replied laughingly, "Sit still or you'll have only yourself to blame if the scissors slip!"

Had the imposter stabbed the real Caroline with those same scissors during a haircut—the braid!—and somehow managed to make it appear accidental? Ida Kate rubbed her eyes. Nothing made sense.

"This is a fine job," Papa said appreciatively when the haircut was over and the false Caroline handed him the small mirror. "You must have had a lot of practice. I expect you learned by cutting your husband's hair?"

"Yes, indeed, whenever Claude needed it. The last thing I want to see across my table is a shaggy ape of a man! I guess little Hanky will come in for his share of trims, but not yet. Those sweet red curls are just right—"

"Clivedon," Ida Kate interrupted loudly.

They stopped talking and turned to her. "*Clivedon,* not Claude," Ida Kate said. Her hands were sweating, and she punched them into the pockets of her pinafore. She felt the dagger there, and the letter. The recipe. The photograph. "Your husband's name was *Clivedon* Fairchild— at least that's what you wrote to us."

Her father just stared at her. But the woman at his side

grew pale. Then she shook her head ruefully at Ida Kate. "Of course I said Claude, my dear. It was Clivedon's middle name—the one his family always used. But he preferred Clivedon for business purposes. Thought it sounded more prestigious." She smiled and turned back to Papa.

"Now, hold it right there, Henry, my dear. There's just a little bit at the back here that's uneven . . ." The scissors clicked. She looked over at Ida Kate across Papa's bent head, and her expression was triumphant. "There now. Perfect!"

Chapter 11
False Spring

Ida Kate was running along the trail to school—no, it was the path to the graveyard. There was Mama, waving to her! There was Papa, calling her name! She raced along and the sun was warm and the sky was blue and her feet lifted her so high that soon she was floating along. Yes, she was flying now, flying toward Mama and Papa, brimming with warm happiness because at last they would all be together again . . .

But who was that? Up ahead, next to Papa, another woman waved to Ida Kate. It was a tall, thin woman with a long red braid coiled about her head. She held Hanky. They were both waving—and Mama was fading, as day turned to darkness. Mama was gone, and Caroline Fairchild—the real Caroline Fairchild—stood next to Papa. But not for long—because there behind Papa came *another* woman . . . She came sneaking along, and

Ida Kate knew what the others did not know: it was the impostor, and she was coming to kill Caroline.

"No!" Ida Kate tried to shout a warning, but the sound came out a grunt, like a pig's. "Stop—look behind you, Papa!" she tried to cry. She saw the impostor raise her arm high—she saw the dagger in the impostor's hand, poised to strike! "Caroline! Papa! Hanky!" screamed Ida Kate, and she tried to run to help them, but her legs wouldn't move. She just floated, slow as molasses, above the path.

Then Caroline faded away, and so did the baby. And so did the impostor. Papa was left alone. Ida Kate felt his loss and her own wash over her like a wave, and she started to cry.

The dream girl was crying and the girl in the bed was thrashing from side to side. All night Ida Kate had been tortured by one awful nightmare after another. Now she was finally awakened by a gust of air blowing across her face like a splash of cold water. She gasped in relief and opened her eyes. She was in her bed in the storeroom, with morning light seeping through the cracks around the door.

The door was closed, so where had the cold breeze come from? Ida Kate remembered with a stab of longing her mother's cool hand soothing her forehead after other bad dreams.

"Mama?" she whispered. But there was no answer.

The quilt was twisted tightly around her legs. No wonder she'd felt she couldn't run.

Ida Kate burrowed down into her pillow, wishing to hibernate. But then, from the main room, she heard Papa's laugh and Hanky's high-pitched shriek of delight. She heard the impostor's voice—not sounding half so southern as it had the day before—and she shivered, remembering her dream.

She must try to speak to Papa alone. Today—before he went out to work in the fields—she must tell him what she had figured out. She would show him the photograph and the different handwriting samples. She would open the tin and show him the braid. He would have to believe her! He would take the false Caroline to the depot and put her on the first train leaving Hays City.

But what about Hanky? Would the impostor take the baby away? Ida Kate was stabbed by the same sense of loss she'd felt in her dream. The truth was, she wanted Hanky to stay.

The truth is, you want them both to stay.

Was that Mama's angel voice in her head? Ida Kate scrubbed her fingers into her hair, hard. Well, Mama was wrong this time, even if she was an angel. *Of course I don't want a killer in our house, Mama!*

Ida Kate jumped out of bed and wrapped her shawl around her shoulders. She opened the storeroom door and stepped into the main room.

It was warmer there. Papa, with Hanky on his lap, was finishing his breakfast of eggs and mush and bread. The false Caroline sat across from them. She smiled uncertainly at Ida Kate. "I was just going to come wake you, dear," she said. "So you could say good-bye."

Relief washed over Ida Kate like a warm rain—but mixed with a gust of sorrow, too. "You're leaving us!" It *was* the best solution, she told herself. This way there wouldn't have to be any nasty accusations; this way the impostor bride would simply disappear out of their lives. But then why was some part of Ida Kate crying out, *How can you do this to me?*

"Leaving us?" Papa sounded surprised. "Of course not. I'm the one who has to leave, I'm afraid." He set Hanky down on his blanket on the floor and stood up. "I'm off to Hays City for the day. Got to buy a new plow blade—the other one broke yesterday, darn thing. And I can't work without it. I'll be back in time for supper, or at least I hope I will." He glanced out the window, worry creasing his brow. "If the weather holds."

"Oh, Papa, may I go with you?" begged Ida Kate. "Please, I'd love a day in town. I have to talk to you—" She broke off as Papa shook his head.

"No, my sweet potato. I've got people to see and buying to do, and you've got school. You've been back only a few days, and there's no sense missing any more than you already have."

A swirl of wind outside threw pebbles and dirt from the yard against the windowpanes. The gust rattled the door on its hinges.

"Goodness mercy!" cried the impostor. "And here I thought it was spring in Kansas!"

"It was what we call a false spring," Papa explained. "We often get some very nice warm weather just after Easter, and it lulls everyone into thinking it's safe to unpack the warm-weather garments and fold away all the woolens. But the false spring lasts only a week or two—then the masquerade is over and winter's back."

Unlike the false spring, the false bride was still with them. "*Please,* Papa! Take me with you." Ida Kate felt she couldn't bear having to spend the afternoon alone with the impostor. When would *this* masquerade be over?

"No, dear," Papa said firmly. Again he peered out the window. "Looks like a real storm is brewing, but if I hurry, I should get to town and back before the snow comes."

His words made Ida Kate's stomach clench. Ever since Mama's death, Ida Kate had hated snow. She hated the smallest fluttering of lacy flakes just as much as she hated the huge mounding drifts. She hated early autumn flurries just as much as late spring surprise blizzards. She wished Papa would not leave, but he was struggling into his great-coat now. He kissed her on the cheek, promising to be home as soon as he could. He bent down and touched the top of the baby's red curly head. Then he held out one hand to the impostor.

She placed her hand in his, and he raised it slowly to his lips. "Till we meet again, my lady," he said with teasing gallantry, but his eyes were earnest.

"Godspeed, my good sir," she replied lightly. And then he was gone in a burst of frigid wind, and the door slammed shut behind him.

Ida Kate whirled around and ran back into the darkness of the storeroom, ignoring the woman who called herself Caroline, who was urging her to come back and sit down and eat a proper breakfast.

Ida Kate dressed quickly in her warm flannel dress and black woolen stockings. She had hoped not to need these stockings again until autumn—but the false spring was over. She tied on her pinafore, checking that her evidence was safely in the pockets. She laced her sturdy walking shoes. Her stomach was still clenched tightly, and she knew there was no way she could eat a thing under the impostor's appraising eyes.

There had been that quick moment of elation when Ida Kate thought the false Caroline was saying good-bye, was leaving them this very morning. Then the sinking realization that it was Papa, not Caroline, on his way to Hays City. But if the impostor could be *made* to leave of her own accord . . .

It would spare Papa the heartache of knowing the truth.

Ida Kate stepped out of the chilly storeroom and closed the door behind her. The false Caroline stood by the table with the frying pan. "Would you like one egg or two, dear?"

Ida Kate took a deep breath, summoning her courage. With her eyes she measured the distance between where she stood and the door to the yard—a mere five paces. It was now or never. Never mind that this was the same woman who had brought laughter and song back into their home. *Never mind,* Ida Kate told herself firmly. *You can't have it both ways.* It was time to take a stand.

"I know you aren't Caroline Fairchild!" Ida Kate's accusation burst out like a gunshot. "You're somebody named Lucy—"

The woman gasped.

"There's no use pretending," Ida Kate continued, outrage making her voice grow louder and colder with every word. But why were tears streaming down her face as well? "You thought to trick us, but I've figured you out. You're a liar and a kidnapper!" She dashed the tears away with her hand. "*And* a murderess!"

The impostor looked stunned. She set down the pan and moved toward Ida Kate, hands outstretched. Ida Kate ran to the door and wrenched it open. She backed out the door into the wind. Every pore of her body was tingling with panic, with triumph, with despair.

"Wait! Ida Kate, you come back in here!" cried the

woman who was not Caroline Fairchild.

Ida Kate hugged her school slate to her chest. "Just pack up now and go!" she screamed at the impostor. "I don't want you marrying Papa. I have proof! You can be sure that soon *everyone* will know of your crimes."

The impostor staggered toward Ida Kate. She pressed her hands to her face—"Oh, no, Ida Kate, no! You can't believe . . . Oh, surely you don't believe that!"—and burst into tears. Then she turned and ran through the house to her bedroom.

Ida Kate turned and ran in the other direction. She ran as fast as she could, head down, legs pumping along the trail to school. She was angry and victorious—surely the impostor's tears proved her guilt!

She did not stop for Martha. Her anger propelled her on past the Ruppenthals' farm, on past the turnoff to Hays City where her father was, even now, riding farther and farther away from her. The sky was darkening steadily, and the wind blew even colder than before. By the time Ida Kate arrived at school, wispy snowflakes began drifting across the prairie.

The first hour of school passed slowly, and the children were distracted by the wind rattling the windowpanes. No one could recall the oceans of the world. Finally Miss Butler stepped outside. She was back in seconds, announcing breathlessly that she would close school for the day. "We'll be snowed in here, if those flakes keep piling up so fast. But if you all set off now, you'll get home safely before it turns into a real blizzard."

The teacher gave Martha, the twins, and Ida Kate a ride in her wagon as far as the turnoff. The twins raced on ahead, and the girls followed. Ida Kate had to take deep breaths to keep at bay the panicky feeling that snow always caused in her. She could see all too well in her mind's eye how Mama had looked when they'd brought her in from the snow. No one would ever know why Mama had wandered outside into the blizzard while Ida Kate and Papa were in the barn tending the animals. Perhaps her fever had made her delirious. It had been nearly an hour before Papa and Ida Kate found her by the barn, snowflakes melting on her hot skin, her hair frosted with a lacy veil of ice. She'd grown sicker that night, and yet the doctor could not be summoned. Mama had never recovered from that illness. She was dead before the three-day blizzard was over.

As Ida Kate walked with Martha toward the Ruppenthals' farm, she thought she could hear Mama's voice in her head reciting lines from their favorite Whittier poem about the snowstorm:

> *Unwarmed by any sunset light*
> *The gray day darkened into night,*
> *A night made hoary with the swarm*
> *And whirl-dance of the blinding storm.*

The words rang in Ida Kate's mind as if Mama had really spoken them. She felt so strange . . . as if something were just waiting to happen. It was the sudden snowstorm making her feel this way, Ida Kate told herself, and also the unpleasant scene that morning. She was unsettled, that was all. She heard Mama's angel voice calling to her now: *Hurry home, my sweet girl!*

Ida Kate walked faster. She took Martha's arm as they hurried along and told her what had happened that morning.

"You mustn't go home," Martha told Ida Kate. "Because with this snow, she probably hasn't left yet. What if she's still there—waiting for you? You could be in terrible danger. Stay with us, Ida Kate, until your father comes."

It was sound advice, but as Ida Kate pressed on through the falling snow, her mind replayed the scene at their house that morning, and she saw again the shocked expression on the impostor's face; she remembered again how the woman had staggered, how she'd gasped at the accusation of murder, how she'd cried out, "Surely you don't believe that!"

As Ida Kate walked with Martha at her side, snow began swirling in blinding sheets around them, and she remembered other things: The impostor's lovely voice singing hymns or crooning lullabies to the baby. Her gentle hands crimping pie pastry, or making the perkiest hair bows from even the limpest ribbons, or altering her

own pretty dress to fit Ida Kate. Her excitement over
Ida Kate's favorite kitten, Millie. How often Papa laughed
now that his mail-order bride had come . . .

Martha's excited voice chattered on in Ida Kate's ear,
though the two friends could barely see each other now
in the blizzard. "Remember the dagger, and the hair!
Remember the lies! And how she killed that snake with
a single blow!"

Ida Kate *was* remembering that single blow—how
quickly the impostor was there to save the baby, how she
didn't flinch from the deadly rattler but struck swiftly,
keeping everyone safe.

Ida Kate heard Mama's voice again now as Mama had
always said in the past: *Know your own mind, my sweet girl.
Keep your own counsel.* And as she walked through the snow,
Ida Kate felt a pinprick of conscience. Could it be she had
let Martha's version of things take over? It would not be
the first time she had followed Martha's lead even when
her own nature cautioned her to behave differently. Mama
used to chide her, in fact, for going along with Martha's
boisterous games and wild schemes.

At the Ruppenthals' house, Ida Kate let go of Martha's
arm. Mama's words had strengthened her. "I'll be all
right," she told her friend, hoping it would be true. "But
I've got to go home."

"Don't be crazy, Ida Kate! You know she's an impostor
and a killer!"

"I know she's an impostor," Ida Kate agreed. "But that's all I know for sure." And she waved good-bye and struggled on toward home.

Hurry home! Hurry home!

The snow was a sheet of white, and the wind swirled the sheet around her, up and over like a heavy petticoat twisting on the clothesline. It was hard to see, but Ida Kate ran her hand along the wire of the Ruppenthals' fence that connected to her own fence, her hand bumping up and down again whenever it passed over one of the limestone fence posts. At last she arrived home—though she could scarcely make out the house through the snow. How simple it would be, she reflected uneasily, to wander in the wrong direction, bearings lost.

A muffled bark startled her. "Hickory!" she shouted. The dog, his shaggy hair matted with snow, crawled out from behind the woodpile where he had been sheltering. "Poor boy!"

Outside the house, Ida Kate could hear Hanky crying even over the wind and through the thick sod walls. She lifted the latch and stepped inside, and a billow of snow followed her. She pushed the door closed with difficulty and latched it. She didn't know what sort of greeting she could expect from the false Caroline after the morning's scene, but she felt determined now to give her a fair chance to explain. Mama would want her to.

"Hello . . ." she called out. "Caroline?" She let the shivering dog come in and hurried through the house, nearly stumbling over Millie, who twined herself around Ida Kate's feet. "*Lucy!*" Ida Kate called again and again. But no one was home except Hanky, who screamed for her from the bedroom. She found him standing in his crib, desperately wailing. The whole house was chilly; the fire was out.

Caroline wasn't there.

Ida Kate's first thought as she comforted the baby was that the impostor had indeed packed her bags and left. Certainly Martha would have said that's what happened, and good thing, too. Good riddance to bad rubbish.

But Ida Kate was thinking more clearly now than she had been since the bride arrived, and she knew that no matter who the impostor really was, she cared about Hanky and would not have left him alone. A quick glance around the bedroom convinced Ida Kate that their visitor was still with them. Her trunk was in the corner by the window, and her dresses hung on the hooks. In the main room, her apron hung on the peg by the stove. But her coat was gone.

Surely she wouldn't go out in this blizzard! Ida Kate told herself. But maybe she had gone to check on the animals and couldn't find her way back from the barn? Ida Kate bundled Hanky up in his quilt and bit back a cry of panic as she ventured out into the swirling white with him in her arms. It was madness to take a baby out into this weather—but he'd been so frightened, left on his own, it would be cruel to walk out on him. And after all, they were going only as far as the barn.

"Don't cry," she told him. "It will be all right." She wished desperately that she could believe what she was saying.

It was now impossible to see anything at all. The wind howled in her ears, and the icy flakes stung her skin. Ida Kate shifted the baby in her arms and stooped to grab hold of the old rope Papa kept tied between the house and the barn all winter; how lucky for her that he had not taken it down yet. Several times in bad storms like this one, they had needed the rope to find their way between the house and the barn. Carefully pulling her way along the rope, Ida Kate finally arrived at the barn. She heaved open the door and slipped inside. Her father had taken Thunder and the mare, Philly; their stalls were empty. The two cows mooed at her, but she could not stop to tend them now. The pigs grunted, but she could not stop to feed them.

Caroline was not there.

Ida Kate's breath felt tight in her chest. Her fear of the snowstorm was wound up inside her. She told herself

what she really should do was just run back to the house,
build up the fire, and sit with Hanky on her lap until Papa
returned. She had wanted the impostor to leave—and
the woman was gone. So Ida Kate should be *glad.*

But she was not glad. She felt that the knot inside
her would never unwind—she would never breathe freely
again—until she found the missing bride. Again the
vision of Mama after they'd found her out in the blizzard
flashed in Ida Kate's memory, and she knew she could
not let Caroline—or whoever she was—stay lost in a
prairie blizzard if there was any way at all to find her.
Ida Kate shifted the heavy bundle of Hanky and struggled to untie the tight knot at the end of the guide rope.
Then, clutching the baby, she followed the rope back
to the house.

Inside, she quickly set the baby in his crib and tossed
in some of the Noah's ark animals for him to play with.
"Sorry," she told him. "But I'll be back soon."

I hope, she thought fearfully, gasping as she opened
the door and the wind nearly knocked her down. She
dragged the door shut behind her and picked up the rope
again. Now she started walking away from the house,
away from safety, pulling the rope taut as she went. She
was walking in the radius of a circle, shouting out into
the wind: "Caroline! Caroline! Caroline!"

Only the roar of the wind answered her. She had to
walk with her head down, but that didn't matter—it was

impossible to see anything anyway. She called for Caroline
until she was hoarse, but heard no response. Then she
tripped over something covered with snow.

A body? Caroline's frozen body?

But no, it was only the wicker laundry basket, filled
with snow-coated sheets. Caroline—Lucy—must have
been out here, Ida Kate realized. Why had she left the
basket?

Walking on, Ida Kate called out again and again.
Finally she heard an answering cry. She could make out
a shadowy figure ahead through all the white. Caroline!

Ida Kate reluctantly dropped the end of the rope—
her line to safety—and struggled on through the wind
and snow without it. She followed the cry and at last
reached Caroline standing in the snow, holding fast to
one of the limestone fence posts at the edge of the
Demings' property.

"Ida Kate! Oh, I've never been so glad to see anyone
in my whole life!" Caroline hugged her in relief.

"I've been searching and searching," Ida Kate said,
and tears welled in her eyes, only to freeze on her cheeks.
She had to shout to hear her own words.

"I'm frantic about Hanky," Caroline gasped, pressing
her head against Ida Kate's. "He's alone—oh, Ida Kate,
the poor little lamb alone all this time!"

"I found him. He's all right." Ida Kate spoke right into
Caroline's ear.

"Oh, thank the Lord. It seems I've been out here forever."

The swift, swirling snow obscured everything around them, even the fence post right where they stood. Ida Kate pulled her heavy shawl tighter with fingers that felt like lead. They turned together and struggled back the way Ida Kate had come, toward the rope she'd had to drop. Ida Kate looked for her footprints, but they were obliterated already. The guide rope was also lost under the fast-falling snow.

Over the howling wind, Caroline shouted that she had gone out to the yard to bring in the laundry that had been hanging out all night. Some of it had blown away. She'd started searching for the missing garments—and soon was lost in the blinding snow. Ida Kate could hardly hear the words over the wind, and snow crusted on her eyelids and in her mouth every time she lifted her head.

Caroline stumbled in the snow, and Ida Kate steadied her. The woman was sobbing as she walked, gasping out her story—how she'd headed back toward the house but couldn't see it. How she'd started walking the other way— until she realized she had gone too far. How she'd been desperate to get back to the baby. "But I just couldn't get my bearings," she cried. Another gust of wind threw snow in their faces.

Ida Kate was numb. She could barely see. And what if this wasn't the right way back to the house? It seemed they had been walking a year already. Surely they should be there by now . . . They pressed on as the wild giant that was this snowstorm dumped drifts all around them. She tried to warm herself by picturing a fire—a hot fire blazing in the safe haven of their little house. Her teeth were chattering now, and her feet were completely numb. But there was a warmth, too, in the place where only shortly before the knot of fear had been. A thawing, she realized, was already under way, and had been since the moment she decided to search for the mail-order bride.

The panic was gone, too, even though the snow still swirled dangerously around them. Here she was—out in a blizzard like the one that had killed her mother, out with a woman who was not who she said she was. And yet the fear was gone. It didn't make sense. Nothing made sense but that they had to plow on together in hopes of reaching the house.

Fire, Ida Kate told herself. *Think of fire. Hot tea. Stew in the pot . . .* She said it aloud: "Imagine sitting indoors, safe and warm by the stove. We've got to get Hanky . . . We should be there by now . . ."

And then, like an answer to their prayers, a black shape loomed out of the white. Another few steps and they would have smacked into the side wall of the house. "We're home!" Ida Kate exulted, her heart thudding with gladness.

"Thanks to you," Caroline said. "And when we're inside, *really* sitting by that stove, I believe I know a story you need to hear." Her next words were nearly whipped away in the wind, but still Ida Kate heard them: "A story *I* dearly need to tell, God help me."

CHAPTER 12

STORY TIME

J ust as they'd worked their way around the side of the house and reached the door, a shrouded figure appeared out of the swirling white. It was Papa, covered from head to toe with snow.

Ida Kate threw her arms around him. "Papa!"

"Get inside, quick!" he shouted urgently.

"I was worried about you, Papa!"

"I never made it to Hays City," he explained as they tumbled inside and the fury of the storm blew a drift of snow in with them. Papa slammed the door. They all stood in silence for a moment, sheltered at last, listening to the storm outside.

Ida Kate drew a deep, shaky breath. *Safe!*

Then Hanky's wail broke the silence. Caroline ran to the bedroom.

"I realized that if I didn't hurry home, I might be

stranded in town for days," Papa said, unwrapping Ida Kate's shawl and shaking out the snow. "And it doesn't look like I'm going to need that plow blade as soon as I'd thought I would!" He shook his dark head, and more clumps of snow fell to the floor. "The storm came on so fast, it was all I could do to turn the wagon around and head on home again. Had to walk the horses the last few miles—couldn't even see to ride. I pressed on home, but thought I'd have to sleep in the barn with the animals." He frowned at Ida Kate. "Couldn't find the guide rope—"

"Oh, Papa—that's because I untied it," Ida Kate confessed.

"She came searching for me, Henry," Caroline explained in an unsteady voice, returning with the baby in her arms. "Oh, this has been a terrible adventure, but we're all here, and the important thing now is to build up the fire in the stove and get warm and dried. And comfort this desperate, abandoned baby. Ida Kate, please take him while I change."

"Poor Caroline, what happened to you?" Papa's eyes widened as he took in her appearance for the first time. "Your hair—it's completely frozen! How long have you been outside? And why—?"

"An hour or two, I imagine," Caroline admitted. She was rubbing her hands to get some warmth into them. "Though I must say it seemed many hours more than that to me."

"I want to hear the whole story," Henry said.

"Oh, you will," Ida Kate assured him. "And another story besides, right, *Caroline Fairchild*?"

Papa heard her tone and looked from his daughter to his intended bride, then back again. For the first time he seemed to notice there was tension in the air along with relief at being out of the blizzard. "What's happened here?" he asked. "What's wrong?"

"I promised Ida Kate a story, and she shall have it," Caroline said.

"Story?" he asked. "I'm all in favor of stories around the stove on a day like this!"

They poked up the fire in the oven and left the door open. The orange glow made Ida Kate feel warmer already. Then they settled the baby and changed out of their wet clothes. They warmed milk for Hanky and made hot tea for themselves. Finally they were all warm and dry and wrapped in blankets. Papa cradled Hanky on his lap. The little boy was exhausted. His head lolled comfortably on Papa's shoulder. Old Hickory lay at their feet.

Caroline sat cupping her hot mug of tea with both hands. She stared into it as if attempting to read her fortune in the tea leaves.

Papa watched her, his eyes twinkling. For a long moment, no one spoke. They listened to the howl of the wind and the crackle of the fire. Then Papa cleared his throat. "Once upon a time . . . ?" he asked gently.

Caroline's head jerked up, and she stared at him. But she didn't say a word, and after another moment, she lowered her head again and stared into her cup.

Ida Kate could not sit quietly for much longer. "I'll tell the story if you won't," she said. "But—oh, Papa— you're not going to like it." She took a sip of tea and burned her tongue. "Once upon a time there was a bride. But she *wasn't* who she said she was . . ." Ida Kate stopped. The fake Caroline Fairchild gazed back at her. Then she nodded as if to say, *Do what you have to do.*

"Go on," ordered Papa.

Ida Kate abandoned telling it as a story and just blurted out the words. "Listen, Papa, I'm sorry as anything to have to tell you this. But you mustn't marry Caroline. You won't want to when you know! She's *not* who she says she is—she's *not* Caroline Fairchild!" She saw the impostor droop lower over her tea mug and decided not to mention the murder yet. She wasn't so sure about that part of the story now anyway.

Papa sighed and shook his head. His black beard quivered. He reached over and put his hand on Ida Kate's knee, but his eyes were on the impostor. "I know that, Ida Kate," he said.

The impostor's head flew up. She and Ida Kate were both staring at him.

"I guessed that some time ago," Papa said calmly.

"Y—you did?" Ida Kate was amazed. "But then—well, who is she? Who?"

"I thought you were going to tell me," he said.

"She's somebody named Lucy," Ida Kate whispered. She looked at the impostor, who was slowly nodding her head. "*Lucy*. But—*why?*"

"Why don't we ask her to tell us?" Papa said simply. He turned to the impostor. "My dear, it's story time."

The woman who was Lucy stared at him. Two bright red patches stained her cheeks. Slowly she lowered her head to her hands. Just when Ida Kate opened her mouth to break the awful silence herself, the woman raised her head again. Her eyes were glistening with tears.

"My name is Lucy," she affirmed in a shaky voice. "Lucy Dotson. Just a farm girl from New York, not a belle from North Carolina—nor even South Carolina. I've never been to the South at all, and let me tell you, it will be a relief not having to put on that accent anymore." Her voice broke in a sob.

Ida Kate saw her father's lips twitch in his beard. Her own lips were pressed tightly together against the sobs she felt rising in her throat. Why should she cry? Finally they were hearing the truth! Or were they? How could they believe anything this impostor had to say—ever?

"I went off to work in the factory in Lynn, Massachu-setts," Lucy Dotson was saying in a low, controlled voice. "I lived in a boardinghouse. I shared a room with another factory worker."

"Caroline Fairchild?" whispered Ida Kate.

"Caroline was my friend. But . . ." Lucy Dotson's voice faltered. "She died."

"Don't you mean you *killed* her?" interrupted Ida Kate, the tightness in her throat making her voice tremble. "Why else did you cry and run when I accused you?"

"No," Lucy insisted in a low, intense voice. "I cried because although I already knew you suspected me of not being Caroline, I never dreamed you suspected me of *murder.* I ran to the bedroom and shut myself in when I realized how completely despicable you find me." Then she looked into Ida Kate's eyes. "I was amazed when you came to search for me in the snow—feeling as I know you do. I hoped if I stayed by the fence post someone driving along the track might eventually find me . . . if I managed to last that long. I never once expected *you* would be the one to come searching, Ida Kate, knowing what you think of me . . ."

"But—" Ida Kate began in confusion.

Her father cut her off with a tap on the knee. "Here, why don't you hold this bundle of baby for a bit? You look like you need something to hang on to just now." He passed the sleeping little boy to her. Then he pulled

a clean handkerchief from his vest pocket and handed
it to Lucy.

Ida Kate rested her cheek against Hanky's silky curls.
Lucy wiped her eyes and blew her nose. The fire popped
and the blizzard raged.

"Caroline and I became fast friends," Lucy explained.
"We worked long hours side by side, with the banging of
the machinery and the hiss of the steam engines in our
ears all day. We talked about our lives, about what had
brought us to Lynn. So I learned a bit about Caroline's
family, how they'd lost everything in the war, and how
her brothers and her father had died. I learned how she'd
married a distant cousin who was always something of
an invalid, how she was left widowed with Hanky to
support . . . And I was there when Caroline first decided
to reply to a newspaper advertisement from a Kansas
farmer."

She raised her eyes and gazed at Papa. "We spoke
about how you appeared to be a man of fine character.
How your daughter sounded very sweet. I was happy for
Caroline when she decided to travel to Kansas, though
it would mean losing my dear friend's daily company.
She was so glad to have this chance to get away from the
factory, and to secure a family for little Hanky. She loved
him so much—she would do anything for him, even if it
meant marrying a man she'd never met. I felt glad for her.
She was starting a new life—and a big adventure. I told

her I might well answer such an advertisement myself if a similar one caught my eye. I, too, was longing for adventure . . ."

Her voice trailed off. Papa stroked his beard, staring at the fire. Ida Kate hugged the sleeping baby—Caroline's true son.

But how had he come to be in the care of Lucy Dotson?

As if Lucy had heard Ida Kate's thoughts, she continued her tale. "So Caroline was making her plans, getting ready for her journey to Kansas. Until one terrible day . . ." Her voice faltered. "One day there was a dreadful accident at the factory, and Caroline was . . . killed."

"How?" whispered Ida Kate.

Lucy regarded her for a long moment. "I don't believe you want to know the details of that horrible death, Ida Kate, my dear. There was an explosion—one of the steam boilers . . ." She closed her eyes for a moment as if to blot out the remembered sight of the accident.

Lucy continued her account of the days following Caroline's death. She paid money from her own meager wages to board Caroline's son for another few weeks with his baby minder until it could be decided what would become of him. She'd had to sell most of Caroline's belongings to pay for the funeral, and immediately afterward the landlady of the boardinghouse asked Lucy to clear out the rest of Caroline's things from their room, seeing as there was no family coming to collect them. She needed to rent that bed to the new girl, hired to replace Caroline.

Lucy bit her lip. "The factory conditions are terrible," she muttered. "And the wages are pitiful. But the factory owners can always hire another girl to replace one who leaves—or dies. People are lining up every day in the cities, desperate for work."

It was while she sorted through Caroline's belongings that Lucy found the packet of letters from Henry Deming. "Caroline had saved every one of them," she told Papa, lifting her head and looking straight at him. "You should know that she treasured them."

"And you read them," he said, his voice stern.

Lucy flinched from his tone, but nodded. Ida Kate shifted in her chair. She was beginning to see how everything had happened. "You read them," she said to Lucy, "and decided—"

"I decided," Lucy interrupted in a stronger voice, "to read every one. Caroline had already shared the first one with me, but then I read the rest. I confess it freely, though I know it was not my place to read them. They were delightful—a bright spot in the difficult task of sorting through everything of Caroline's. I often imagined I could hear her laughter and feel her presence near me as I read the letters." Lucy turned to Ida Kate. "As you say you feel your mama, my dear. A happy, loving presence."

"Yes," murmured Ida Kate. "That's how it is." She shifted the baby in her arms and carefully sipped her tea. Papa was still staring into the fire, silent.

"Everything—I had to sort through all her most personal things," continued Lucy after a moment. "I had to decide what to save and what to sell or give away. I gave her clothing to factory girls who wore the same size. I gave many of her books and trinkets to her other friends, but I kept some things for Hanky. For when he's older. His father's dagger. And something of his mother's . . ."

"Her hair?" breathed Ida Kate.

Papa turned from the fire, shooting Ida Kate a puzzled look. But Lucy nodded. "Yes, I cut off the braid after the funeral, before the burial. Caroline had such lovely hair—and even though she was dead, that braid still looked so alive! I thought that someday Hanky might be glad to have it. A little bit of his mother . . ."

Papa's stern expression softened as he smiled at Lucy. "That was kind of you," he said. "I did the same thing when Eleanor died. I cut a lock of her hair to remember her by."

"Papa, you *did?*" Ida Kate had not known that.

He turned his smile on Ida Kate. "I take it you found this braid of Caroline's and thought . . ."

She flushed. "Yes." She looked at Lucy. "I'm sorry. I should have known you weren't a murderess."

Lucy studied her for a moment, and tears started
to well in her eyes again. "You're a generous girl,
Ida Kate." She cleared her throat and resumed her
story.

"I read all the letters, and I was struck by how interesting you both were—you, Henry, and Ida Kate, too.
The letters were lovely, Henry, and . . ." She hesitated,
then lowered her eyes miserably. "And I rather think
I fell in love." She took a deep breath and looked up
again, meeting Papa's eyes. "I decided I would write to
you immediately and tell you what had befallen your
intended bride. But then I saw the train ticket."

She drained the last drops of her tea and set the mug
onto the stove top. She took a deep breath and wiped
her tears with Papa's handkerchief. "I told myself I would
use the ticket to come to Kansas with Hanky. I—I knew
it was wrong, but I had been longing to escape the factory work, yet I didn't want to go back to living with my
brother and his wife who took over our family farm after
my parents died. I wanted a home of my own."

"And Hanky needed a home, too," Ida Kate added,
glancing down at the baby.

"Yes. The landlady was going to take him to the
county orphanage, but I couldn't bear to see that happen.
I said I'd take care of him myself. I thought that's what
Caroline would have wanted. I guess I was telling myself
that I would come with the baby to Kansas and explain

everything when I arrived." She sighed. "But I didn't explain. I know I was terribly wrong."

"You're telling us now," Papa said calmly. Ida Kate stared at him in wonderment. He stretched out his long legs toward the stove. "I wondered why I didn't hear from you—that is, from Caroline—after I'd sent the train ticket. But that must have been about the time she was killed . . ."

Lucy nodded. "So after I decided to go in her place, I packed my things and Hanky's—as well as Caroline's family photograph album. I didn't know who any of the people were, but I thought Hanky might like to have likenesses of his ancestors. Perhaps one of them is his father."

"Clivedon Fairchild," said Ida Kate. "Not *Claude*."

"Not Claude," agreed Lucy. "Clivedon Fairchild, from North Carolina. But, you see, I had only my memories to go on. Where had Caroline said she'd grown up? Did she have any living relatives? What had her family been like? I had her letters from you, so I knew details about who I would be meeting once I got here—but I did not have her letters to you. I didn't know what she'd told you about herself."

"You didn't know she wrote that cats made her sneeze," Ida Kate said.

"Exactly." Lucy patted her lap, and Millie leaped up and curled into a ball.

Papa laughed. "A vital clue."

"There were lots of clues," Ida Kate said. She nuzzled the sleeping baby.

Lucy sighed. "Especially Hanky, I imagine. I—I haven't had much experience with babies . . . maybe you've noticed?"

Ida Kate had to smile. "A little," she said.

"I have no doubt the poor lamb misses Caroline," said Lucy. "I miss her so dreadfully myself."

Papa was grinning at Lucy now. "I never knew a mother to have such trouble dressing a baby," he said. "You've got his sweater inside out, even now."

Lucy blushed. Ida Kate folded back a corner of the blanket around the sleeping boy to peek at the sweater he was wearing. She grinned. "So, Papa, you knew all the time?" She wasn't quite sure how she felt now, knowing the story.

Certainly Lucy's story made more sense of the facts than Martha's dramatic theories of murder had. But . . . this Lucy Dotson was still a liar, even if she wasn't a killer or a kidnapper. Why had Papa not challenged her when he first suspected she was not who she said she was? And how far could they trust that *this* tale was the truth?

"I suspected something was amiss," Papa said calmly. "But I never once—not for one second—suspected Lucy of murder." He hitched his chair closer to Lucy's; he put his hand on her arm. "Lucy, my dear, I could see there was something you wanted to tell me. Over and over, whenever we chanced to be alone, it was right on the tip of your tongue."

"Oh, it *was*," said Lucy with a sudden sob. She dabbed her eyes with Papa's handkerchief. "I am so ashamed. I'm not a liar by nature—though how I can ever hope you'll believe that, I don't know—but once I arrived, I *couldn't* tell you. I just couldn't bear to end my time with you. I started sneaking around, searching for the letters Caroline sent, so I could learn more about who I was supposed to be. Oh, the lies just started spiraling. One turned into another, and there was no end in sight. I knew I couldn't keep it up forever—nor would I want to live that way—but I dreaded telling you. I felt so low, and yet I kept on with the ruse because revealing the truth would mean losing you. Ending it. And it's been so wonderful . . ."

"Ending it?" Papa asked sharply. "Why, woman, our wedding date is only two weeks away! I've already arranged everything with the good Pastor Smiley."

"You would have married me, even suspecting . . . ?" Lucy's voice trembled.

"I knew you would come clean by then," Papa said gently.

"How could you know, Papa?" demanded Ida Kate. "How *could* you know that Caroline—I mean Lucy— would tell you who she really was?"

"Because this young charlatan is a woman of fine

character," Papa said, his voice warm. "And she can turn plain mush into something delicious. *And* kill a rattler with a single blow. *And* bring laughter into our house again. *And* sing like an angel." His dark eyes sparkled at Lucy as he continued.

"She comes from a family of abolitionists, even as I do, and she knows what's right and what's wrong. She would never take her wedding vows under a dead woman's name. She just wouldn't be able to, plain and simple."

"No, I wouldn't," Lucy agreed. "But I was so miserable about having to confess, so sad that we wouldn't be able to marry . . . I was just hanging on to my story as long as I could. It was very selfish of me, and I apologize to you both most humbly." She took a deep, shuddering breath, staring for a long minute at the swirling white outside the windows. "I do feel better now, having it all off my chest, and I will pack my bags and leave as soon as the rails are clear again."

"Nonsense," Papa said. "Poor Caroline is dead, God rest her soul. But Lucy Dotson is alive and well, and these two children need a mother, and I certainly need a wife . . . and I *especially* need a wife named Lucy Dotson."

Lucy turned from the window and met Papa's gaze as he left his chair and knelt in front of her.

"Lucy, will you do me the great honor of marrying me?" he asked.

And as Lucy, laughing and crying, leaned forward to embrace him, Ida Kate started to laugh and cry as well. Her cheeks glowed with welcome warmth despite the howling cold outside, and she moved—with Hanky in her arms—into their hug.

Later that night they all sat together at the trestle table. The blizzard outside seemed to be tapering off, and the wind had dropped. Lucy concocted a quick soup of onions and potatoes in broth, and Ida Kate mashed a potato with milk for Hanky. She also opened one of the jars of applesauce from the storeroom for all of them to share.

They ate their simple meal in the glow of the lamps. Hanky, refreshed from his nap, sat on Papa's lap. Papa alternated between spooning soup into his own mouth and aiming bites of mashed potato at Hanky's. Lucy sat opposite Papa, pale and quiet—as if the afternoon's confession had left her feeling weak. But a smile played around her lips, and her eyes were bright.

Ida Kate looked around at them all and thought, *This is my family.*

A happy thought indeed.

But suddenly Lucy's brow furrowed. "What will people say?" she murmured. "How will I ever explain?"

"What do you mean?" To Ida Kate it seemed all their problems were over now that the questions had been answered, the lies revealed, explained—and forgiven. What could trouble them now?

Lucy stared into her soup bowl as if it might hold a solution to her worries. Then she raised her head. "Oh, Henry! What shall I do? Everyone in Hays City and for miles around expects you to be marrying Caroline Fairchild! How am I ever going to explain myself to the Ruppenthals, and to people like Miss Butler, and—good heavens—to Pastor Smiley himself?" She set down her spoon and spread her hands wide. "How will I ever be accepted by the good people of Hays?"

Papa quirked a dark eyebrow at her. "That, my dear, will no doubt be your next big adventure."

Pastor Smiley was at his officious best. He even managed to smile at the couple standing before him. Two weeks after the blizzard, the weather was balmy again, a fine spring day, though humps of dirty snow still lay about the town, melting slowly in the Kansas sun. The courthouse was full of friends and neighbors and townspeople who just wanted a chance to meet the impostor bride. Before the ceremony started, murmurings and hushed remarks filtered through the crowd. Ida Kate, sitting on the front bench with Hanky in her lap, couldn't help but overhear: "Can you imagine?" "Now she says her name is Lucy Dotson!" "Well, I never!" "And what about that baby?" "I knew all along that something was amiss—didn't you?" "I say she's nothing but an adventuress!" "Well, madam, *I* say there's never been a lovelier bride, and look how Mr. Deming is grinning fit to beat the band! He's never been happier."

Ida Kate glanced up at Lucy to see how she was taking all this, but the bride's eyes were on her groom. Their hands were clasped.

Martha, sitting across the aisle with her whole family, waggled her fingers at Ida Kate. Miss Butler sat primly with her parents. And at last Pastor Smiley began. He spoke of the holy state of matrimony and his hopes that this union would be fruitful. He said, "Dost thou, Lucy Dotson, take Henry Clay Deming to be thy lawfully wedded husband?"

"I do." Lucy's voice was clear and full of joy.

Ida Kate, listening to Lucy's words and Papa's response, felt full of wonder and amazement at the way this riddle had been solved. Now there was no impostor—there was only Lucy, the *real* Lucy, and Ida Kate couldn't wait to get started on their new life together.

"You may now kiss the bride," Pastor Smiley said, and Ida Kate, watching with a big smile on her face and jostling baby Hanky on her shoulder, felt Mama looking down at them with approval. *Many blessings on this family,* Mama was saying. And Ida Kate thought it quite likely that the real Caroline Fairchild was up there with Mama—looking down on them all right now— and smiling, too.

1878

A Peek into
the Past

A lone man waits on the platform of a prairie railroad station.

Although Ida Katc's story is fiction, women really did travel west in the nineteenth century to become brides to men they knew only through letters. "Heart and hand" newspapers in the eastern states printed letters from men who had established homesteads in the West and longed for the help and companionship of a wife. One bachelor's letter in 1853 declared, "I love to think of thee and think that thare is a day a coming when wee will be happy together. I live a lonsom and desolate life."

Sometimes a whole group of men would hire a helper, called a *jobber,* to go east and bring back a shipload or train car of women wanting to marry. One report in 1844 described the arrival of a Mississippi River steamboat carrying 41 women. Even before the brides had left the boat, men on shore were calling to them: "Miss with the blue ribbon on your bonnet, will you take me?" and "Hallo thar, gal with a cinnamon-colored shawl! If agreeable, we will jine!"

These women must have decided that life with an unknown man in possibly primitive living conditions was still better than remaining a spinster. Unmarried women had few options for employment, as Caroline Fairchild and Lucy Dotson discovered. Some unmarried women found work in factories or as schoolteachers, but most spent their lives with parents or married siblings, helping to care for nieces, nephews, and the elderly.

This woman's advertisement for a husband says, "Have had a sad life so far, but have not given up."

Marriage offered women security and a home and children of their own. In the nineteenth century, love was rarely the reason for marriage—though often love grew between a couple after they had married. Instead, both men and women married for companionship, social standing, children, and help in running a home and farm or business.

Many men on the frontier who wanted to marry could not find wives, however. Taming the West was considered a job for men, so there were few single women among the early settlers. In the mid-1870s, for example, there were ten times more men than women in Kansas!

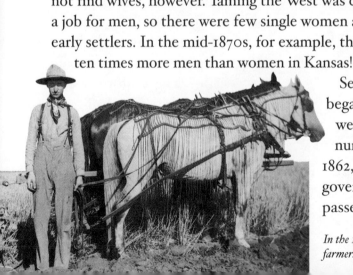

Settlers began heading west in large numbers in 1862, when the government passed the

In the 1870s, many frontier farmers were bachelors.

Posters like this one encouraged hordes of hopeful settlers to move west.

Homestead Act. This law gave 160 acres of land to anyone who paid a $10 filing fee and farmed the land for five years. Ida Kate's father would have been one of thousands who flooded into Kansas, Nebraska, Minnesota, and the Dakotas after the Civil War to claim land of their own.

These settlers included Americans from the East—both white people and freed slaves—as well as immigrants from abroad, like Martha's stepmother. Many were farmers or ranchers, but others were shopkeepers, blacksmiths, wagon makers, dressmakers, saloon owners, innkeepers, doctors, ministers, and teachers who settled in the small towns that dotted the railroad lines.

In the eastern part of the prairies, settlers built log cabins. But in the western prairies, where trees were scarce, some settlers lived in *dugouts*—homes hollowed out of hills. Others, like Ida Kate's family, built sod houses out of "prairie brick," heavy blocks of earth cut straight from the prairie.

Homesteaders on the plains faced fierce challenges—tornadoes, grass fires, hailstorms, floods, and blinding blizzards. Some years vast, crackling

A family poses in front of their sod house.

black clouds of grasshoppers would drift in on the winds, ruining the crops and trying to eat everything else in sight.

Yet the settlements and the settlers managed to hold on. In 1867, the year Ida Kate and her parents moved west, railroad track was just being laid through Kansas. To protect the railway builders from Indian attack, Fort Hays was built along Big Creek, and the town of Hays City sprang up nearby. At first Hays City was just a shantytown of flimsy buildings and tents at the end of the railroad line, and it teemed with "Wild West" adventurers and outlaws. But the railroad soon brought farmers, businessmen, cowboys, and soldiers to the area. As newcomers flooded in, however, the original inhabitants of the prairie were driven out. The buffalo disappeared, and Indian tribes were forced to move south and west. Most of the outlaws and adventurers moved further west, too, following the frontier.

By 1878, the year of Ida Kate's story, Hays City had become a real town centered along one wide street a few blocks long. Like most prairie towns, it was the hub of frontier society. People from miles around would meet at the general store or at church. The town sometimes

The main street of Hays City in 1879

seemed rough and lawless, but most frontier families loved its bustle and energy. Farm women tried to go into town every few weeks for shopping, sewing circles, church picnics, and even literary societies.

Most frontier girls and women, like Ida Kate and Lucy, were used to the hard work involved in housekeeping and farming. But women raised in cities or in wealthy families, like Caroline Fairchild, would have found life on the

Kansas ladies gather for a sewing circle in 1899.

prairie more challenging. Such women were no strangers to hard times, however. The decades following the Civil War were difficult all over America, but especially in the South, where many once-wealthy families found themselves nearly penniless. Women who had been raised in luxury, like Caroline, had to find jobs for the first time.

Many people desperate for work headed to the factories and mills of Massachusetts, just as Caroline and Lucy did. Factory work was hard and dangerous, with long hours and meager pay, but it was steady work. Children were paid very low wages, and women earned only slightly more—less than half of what men earned. Because of this, greedy factory owners preferred to hire women and children instead of men. Unmarried women workers lived in cramped, crowded boardinghouses near the mills.

Women in this Lynn, Massachusetts, factory spent long hours sewing shoes and boots in crowded, noisy conditions.

The shoe factory in Lynn, Massachusetts, where Caroline and Lucy worked, was a huge, smoky room where 200 girls and women tended 500 roaring, steam-powered sewing machines. The workers painted glue onto leather, gummed down the edges of seams, and hammered the soles of shoes and boots into place. If their bare hands touched the shoe dyes, their fingernails would rot off from the chemicals. Accidents—explosions, fires, and malfunctioning machines— were all too common.

In the 1870s, the noisy factory towns and bustling cities of the East seemed overcrowded, hopeless places to many. These people—like Ida Kate's family, like Caroline and Lucy—looked to the West, where open land was still plentiful and dreams could stretch across grass-land, deserts, and mountains.

GEOGRAPHICAL NOTE

Castle Rock is a large, dramatic natural rock formation approximately 40 miles west of Hays, Kansas. For the purposes of this story, its location has been moved closer to the Deming farm to allow the Demings to travel there for a picnic. Settlers living close to Castle Rock visited frequently, marveling at its towering height rising from the flat prairie. Castle Rock is still a popular tourist attraction today.

ABOUT THE AUTHOR

Kathryn Reiss grew up near Cleveland, Ohio. When she wasn't dreaming of being transported back to the nineteenth century, she had her nose stuck in a book—usually a mystery. When she couldn't find anything the slightest bit eerie or criminal happening in her neighborhood, she started writing stories about mysteries she *wished* she would uncover.

Now she lives with her husband, three children, two cats, and dog in a 130-year-old house in northern California. They have yet to unmask an impostor, stumble into a secret room, or see even the wispiest ghost—but she has not given up hope!

Her eight previous novels have won many awards. The titles are *Time Windows, Pale Phoenix, The Glass House People, Dreadful Sorry, PaperQuake,* and the Ghost in the Dollhouse trilogy. She teaches writing at Mills College.